Anonymous

**Harriet Anne Lucas, wife of John Lucas, died at her Philadelphia**

**residence**

Anonymous

**Harriet Anne Lucas, wife of John Lucas, died at her Philadelphia residence**

ISBN/EAN: 9783337120856

Printed in Europe, USA, Canada, Australia, Japan

Cover: Foto ©Raphael Reischuk / pixelio.de

More available books at **www.hansebooks.com**

To

# MRS. BERTHA HONORE PALMER,

President

of the

Board of Lady Managers

of the

World's Columbian Exposition, Chicago,

and

Representative of Woman's Work before the World,

This Memorial Volume of the Life and
Public Services of

# MRS. HARRIET ANNE LUCAS,

is by permission
respectfully dedicated.

———

# HARRIET ANNE LUCAS,

wife of John Lucas,

died at her Philadelphia residence,

1913 Arch Street,

May 8th, 1893.

Her singularly noble and useful life, her wide range of practical effort for the best interests of the whole people, her vigor and success in elevating Woman's Work, and her unequaled sweetness and simplicity of personal character, created a wide circle of personal and devoted friends. Much as she had suffered from overwork at intervals for two or three years, all were shocked at the announcement of her death. All felt it as a great public loss, and all felt it keenly as a personal grief.

The tributes of respect and affection sent to her husband on this occasion are

very striking in their earnestness and sincerity. They do honor to their writers, not less than to the object of their sorrow. They have been placed in my hands to properly arrange them in a memorial volume which will express, in addition to these personal tributes, a further and more general history of the noble work of Mrs. Lucas. In arranging them, it appears to me proper to give them the direct order of date as received, and to give in most cases the entire matter of the notes as received.

This body of testimony to Mrs. Lucas' worth will, therefore, have the first place, and following it will be given the best statement of my own knowledge of her singularly great public services first, and of her wonderful power to influence even the Senate of the United States to do acts

of public service which her own genius proposed.

For a period of nearly twenty years I have been honored by her confidence, and permitted to aid her to the best of my ability in these public services, and if no other person had given expression to the honor she had earned before the whole people, I would myself have done so, in order to teach the lesson of high duty as well as of high power on the part of those who have her ability in any degree, or who can, as she did, create the largest opportunities, instead of waiting for them to fall to their hands. And I hope this Memorial will be most widely distributed, and will be taken by the women of this country in the highest sense as a public service, and as a memorial of her personal right to public honor. It would not be

right or just to her memory to limit this testimonial to the single point of her personal worth or the devotion of her personal friends; yet there was not a shadow of formalism or a suggestion of officiousness in all her efforts. She did not seek combinations or committees, or have occasion for the use of many of the usual agencies to influence public bodies. Her own words, direct and unaffected, were more eloquent and more powerful, as I can personally testify, than all the machinery of committees or conventions.

And again it must be said that no hour of public service, nor any one among the hundreds of efforts made by her to do this superior work, ever separated her for a single moment from such devotion to her home, her husband and her family, as gave her equal honor as a leader and

guide in purely personal and social duty. But on this point these earnest and respectful tributes from her immediate personal friends are, perhaps, the best expression.

It is a first duty of those who would do justice to Mrs. Lucas' memory to see that her acts and works in the public service are not forgotten nor neglected. The latest of these, representing her designs and plans for the World's Fair at Chicago, is still a vigorous and living issue. If that Fair is to exercise the wide influence intended by her, the women of Pennsylvania should maintain their active interest in every phase of it. It would be possible to use the County Associations, and their personal agencies, in distributing the practical conclusions reached at the Fair.

Perhaps the most important of these is the proved capacity of woman's direction in these great social advances. It was not a mistake to recognize and establish a Woman's Department, and especially it was not a mistake or an ineffective branch to establish the Pennsylvania Committee of Woman's Work. A vast service to the whole social order has already been rendered by this committee, and it must not be dropped or subordinated as the Fair is brought to a conclusion. The ladies of this committee, remaining in its charge, are less self-assertive, perhaps, than they should be, and it is quite certain that the Governor and the chiefs of the Commission will readily permit the fullest degree of reporting upon Woman's Work as the Fair progresses. The plan having been

laid with such elaborate care and fullness, it cannot be possible that it will fail to be shown in the results as fully as it has done in the outline of design.

It is proper, however, to limit this statement of the general relation Mrs. Lucas held to public affairs, to the changes produced immediately by the shock of her illness and death. The emotions felt by all the circle of her friends, official and personal, were overwhelming at the time. The letters of condolence here given are none of them formal, and none of the acts or resolutions passed by the Boards or Committees are without strong evidence that their authors felt the loss as a great and personal one. It is, therefore, better to limit the present statement to this mere introduction, and to refer those who may read

it to the more extended history of her public career which constitutes the second part of this Memorial.

# Letters of Condolence.

# Letters of Condolence.

The following telegrams and letters of condolence were received at their several dates, as the immediate expression of sympathy and respect of their writers. They are here given, nearly in full, as received :

Harrisburg, Pa., May 9, 1893.

From Robert E. Pattison, Governor :

You have my warmest sympathy in this hour of sad bereavement. The interests of the State have lost in Mrs. Lucas a warm advocate. She made a deep impression by her interest in the silk culture, and by her efforts in behalf of Pennsylvania at the Exposition.

World's Fair Grounds,
Chicago, May 9, 1893.
From A. B. Farquhar, Executive Commissioner :
Accept my heartfelt sympathy in your great misfortune ; your gentle, beautiful wife was dear to us all.

———

Philadelphia, May 9, 1893.
From Rev. Herman L. Duhring :
I have just heard of your dear wife's death, and the loss to you must certainly be a great one, and to the children even greater. But what a record she has left of so many good works for our blessed Master! Truly she went about doing good everywhere, and verily she has gone both to her rest and her reward, in that blessed home where sorrow and sickness are no more a burden.

———

4027 Walnut Street,
Philadelphia, May 10, 1893.
From Bishop O. W. Whitaker :
I beg leave to tell you of my sympathy with you in the great loss you have sustained. I have feared for more than two years that Mrs. Lucas

was overtaxing her strength, and that the Church might soon be deprived of her invaluable aid. Everywhere she will be greatly missed, and everywhere she has been her works will follow her.

With heartfelt remembrance of the good she did, and greatest sympathy with you,

I am, sincerely yours,

O. W. Whitaker.

———

June 30, 1893.

From Bishop A. C. Coxe:

Need I say how much I am pained to learn of the decease of that amiable and remarkable Christian lady, your excellent and exemplary wife? You have the condolence of multitudes whom her life and labors have blessed; and through our common and valued friend, Dr. Ashton, I have learned so much of her life and character that mine is no common tribute of sympathy and regret.

Faithfully yours, in the love of Christ,

A. Cleveland Coxe,

Bishop of Western New York.

Trenton, N. J., May 11, 1893.

From Bishop John Scarborough:

My Dear Mr. Lucas: Though I could not be with you to-day, you have my prayers and sympathy in your great loss and sorrow. I had the most profound reverence and regard for your dear wife's character; she was the most unselfish woman. The sad news of her death was brought to me in the Convention by Mr. Milby, and while I was not wholly unprepared for it, I still find it hard to realize that I will never again hear her greeting or see her face on this side of the veil. She won my admiration, many years ago, as a woman of affairs, and every year my admiration grew. She will be missed as few others would be—your loss of course, the greatest, then the children next. But she filled a large place in the world, and outside the home there will be many an aching void. My own personal obligations to you both have been very large for the generous gift of Church property at Gibbsboro. I wish now that in some way that little Church that she named and loved might be made a memorial of her.

I need not tell you where to look for comfort in this hour; the words of friends, though well

meant, will sound empty. There is but one that can pour balm into your aching heart. Look to Him and He will enable you to bear what He sends.

My wife joins me in messages of love and condolence, and though she did not know Mrs. Lucas as well as I did, yet she knew her well enough to recognize her wonderful power and great goodness. May God comfort you, and strengthen you by His grace to bear what he sends you. Remember me kindly to your children and believe me.

Your friend sincerely,<br>John Scarborough.

---

The Deanery, Denver, Colorado,<br>May 16, 1893.

From Rev. H. Martyn Hart:

My Dear Old Friend: I was thinking of you when the postman put the black-edged letter into my hand, and I felt she had gone. Well, all I pray is, that you and I may be where she of a certainty is. Good, dear, capable and blessed woman! Mrs. Hart wrote two or three months ago, but she got the wrong address, and the letter came back through the dead letter office.

She would like to hear how it all came, from Nellie. But I know that the thread of life gradually wound off the spool and she departed.

I am far more sorry for you—to have such a wife, and then to be without her, is indeed to feel a want. Try to feel she is near you, and try to be and do what she would like you to be. But the heart knoweth its own bitterness, and no other intermeddleth with it, and nothing on earth will make up for your loss. I only hope God will give you help to "go softly" the bit of the way you have left to go, and then we will all soon be there.

My wife, of course, sends her love to you all. She often, often talked of her. She made a great impression on her.

Ever in much sympathy, yours,

H. Martyn Hart.

———

1240 South Broad Street,
Philadelphia, June 27, 1893.

From Rev. James S. Stone:

My Dear Mr. Lucas: I will do as you wish me and have the sermon printed in a form that will please you and all who may read it. I am so glad you liked it. It was my great desire to

say words that in themselves would be worthy of my subject—or to put it in another way, my love for you and yours was such, that I wanted the sermon to be both an exact delineation of Mrs. Lucas, and also as far as I could possibly make it, a finished piece of art. My affection must be understood in my effort.

I would have done more—anything for you that was in my power. God bless you in these sad days, and make still more real the assurance that she is at rest.

Will you kindly fill up the blanks in the enclosed, so that I may add it to the sermon? With love to you all, I remain,

Yours sincerely,

James S. Stone.

————

1224 Chestnut Street,

Philadelphia, May 9, 1893.

From Rev. T. A. Fernley:

You will pardon the liberty taken by a comparative stranger, but my sincere sympathy with you in your great sorrow will be a sufficient apology.

I had the pleasure of some acquaintance with your departed wife. I knew her as a positive

friend of the Christian Sabbath. I admired her for the noble stand she took on the Ladies' Board in favor of Sunday closing of the Columbian Exposition, and I had learned to esteem her as a Christian lady.

Her works do follow her—she has done her part, and has entered upon her great and eternal reward. While you are sitting under the shadow of this great sorrow, may I remind you, my dear brother, that He doeth all things well. You mourn not as those without hope. The beautiful, gone out from your earthly home, has expanded into a better and happier life—in the House not made with hands, eternal in the Heavens.

———

Board of Lady Managers, World's Columbian Commission.

Office of the Secretary,
Chicago, May 10, 1893.

Mr. John Lucas:

Dear Sir: In accordance with the following resolution, adopted by the Executive Committee of the Board of Lady Managers, I have the honor to transmit you herewith a copy of a communication adopted by said committee at

a meeting held May ninth, eighteen hundred and ninety-three.

Most truly yours,

Susan G. Cooke.

Resolved, That a communication conveying suitable expressions of sympathy and regret be sent to Mr. John Lucas, of Philadelphia.

Whereas, Our Heavenly Father, on the eighth day of May, one thousand eight hundred and ninety-three, called to a better world our esteemed colleague, Mrs. Harriet Anne Lucas, of Pennsylvania, who has during previous meetings of our Board, been one of our number, sitting in our councils and taking part in our deliberations; and,

Whereas, It is fitting that we pause at this time to heed the admonitions which are suggested to us by this, another visitation from the messenger of death; and,

Whereas, It is appropriate that we express our appreciation of one who with willing hands has ever been ready to labor for the advancement of her sex, and to carry out in every possible way the plans and purposes of our Board; therefore be it

Resolved, That in the death of Mrs. Harriet Anne Lucas, the Board of Lady Managers of the World's Columbian Commission, has lost one of its most loved and useful members, one who was recognized by all as a high type of Christian womanhood; and further be it

Resolved, That we tender to the bereaved ones our heartfelt sympathy in this their hour of great loneliness.

Resolved, That this tribute to the memory of our loved associate be spread upon our minutes, and an engrossed copy of the same sent to the afflicted family.

Mrs. E. W. Allen,
Mrs. Belle H. Perkins,
Ellen A. Ford.

———

I hereby certify that the foregoing is a true and correct copy of the proceedings of the Executive Committee of the Board of Lady Managers, at its session in Chicago, Illinois, May ninth, one thousand eight hundred and ninety-three.

Witness my hand and the seal of the Board of Lady Managers of the World's Columbian Commission, this ninth day of May, one thousand eight hundred and ninety-three.

Susan G. Cooke,<br>Secretary.

———

At a special meeting of the Women's Silk Culture Association, United States, held Monday, May 22, 1893, the following Preamble and Resolutions were adopted :

Whereas, It has pleased our Heavenly Father, in His Wise Providence, to call from her earthly labors our beloved President, Mrs. Harriet Anne Lucas, who so earnestly and faithfully performed the duties of that office since our organization in 1880, therefore be it

Resolved, That it is with feelings of profound sorrow that we record the death of our dear friend and co-worker, and that we desire to express our sense, not only of official, but of personal loss, in the death of one with whom

we have been so long and so pleasantly associated. We tender our sincere sympathy to her husband and family. We also direct that this minute be entered on our record and a copy be sent to the family, and that it be published.

Mrs. Matthew Simpson,
Mrs. C. D. Thumm,
Mrs. W. B. Eltonhead,
Miss Phœbe Horne,
Mrs. William F. Reynolds,
Mrs. S. G. Flagg,
Vice-Presidents.

Miss S. Benner,
Recording Secretary.

Mrs. C. H. Horne,
Corresponding Secretary.

Mrs. H. P. Taylor,
Treasurer.

Mrs. Jacob Dowler,
Mrs. Joseph Lennig,
Mrs. T. Van Rennselaer Yard,
Members.

Mrs. E. V. B. Osbourne,
Hon. Vice-President.

From A. B. Farquhar,

Executive Commissioner:

Mr. John Lucas: It was good of you to telegraph me. You knew how deeply I would sympathize with you all.

Mrs. Lucas was altogether one of the most lovely women whom it has ever been my good fortune to meet. "To see her was to love her, to know her a liberal education." Her death has cast a gloom upon every one here. Mrs. Palmer has several times asked me about her.

You have your children—one of the loveliest families I have ever been favored to know. But nothing can ever take the place of the wife and the mother. Words of mine can bring no comfort. I am not attempting to offer consolation; but a suggestion I may offer—that is—that you keep occupied, push your business, and everything that will take up your time; and encourage the daughters to be busy at something. Work during the day until tired nature forces sleep at night, and time—the great healer—will eventually soothe.

I am very sincerely your friend,

A. B. Farquhar,
Executive Commissioner.

Harrisburg, May 10, 1893.

John Lucas, Esq.

Dear Sir: Since I have been associated with your wife on the State Columbian Board, I have come to know her so well, and to esteem her so highly, that perhaps in some remote degree I can appreciate what your great sorrow must be. She was so earnest, so sincere, so lovely in disposition and character, that every one who met her must feel her loss, even while believing that she is happier now, being freed from human shackles and human pain.

I have feared for some time that she was working beyond her strength, but I hoped that rest would again restore her energy.

Our entire Board will miss her deeply, and mourn with you with truest sympathy.

Mabel Cronise Jones.

———

Woman's Building,
Chicago, May 8, 1893.

Miss Estelle Russel writes:

It was with the greatest sorrow that I heard to-day, through Mrs. Palmer's secretary, of the

death of dear Mrs. Lucas. I cannot tell how badly I feel. I only wish that I was in Philadelphia, that I might possibly be able to do something. I felt the last time I saw her —the day before I left for Chicago—that she could not last much longer; yet when the worst came, it was such a shock. How every one will miss her! Still we should not grieve, for she was a great sufferer, and is happy now, and at rest.

———

Philadelphia, May 8, 1893.

Mr. Wm. Underdown writes:

I was greatly surprised this morning to hear from Dr. Stone of the death of your beloved wife. Please accept my deepest sympathy (in which my dear wife and daughter will unite) in this hour of sorrow and bereavement ; but try and not think of her as dead, but only gone to her eternal rest, after a life of noble work for the good of others. How many in this City of Brotherly Love, and other places, will remember her affectionately. I will call and see you as soon after the funeral as possible.

Another friend writes:

I heard with sorrow, this noon, of the departure of your beloved. Her earthly cares have at last been brought to a close, to receive that Heavenly blessing she has so well earned. How nobly she bore the cross, and well she deserves the crown! All those who knew her good and kind nature must join in asking God's blessing.

A more fond mother never lived, and with all her family cares she was ever ready to reach out and help lighten the burdens of others, much beyond her physical strength. This earth has certainly parted with a Queen of her sex.

What we look upon as a disaster is, after all, a great promotion. If ever Heaven welcomed a pure and holy spirit the occasion exists now with your beloved. I am reminded now of the consoling lines inserted in this notice, of the departure of my beloved daughter:

The tomb is not a blind alley, it is a thoroughfare;
It closes in the twilight to open on the dawn.

Atlantic City, N. J., May 9, 1893.

Henry Wootton writes:

I have just been informed of the death of your dear wife; no words can make amends for the great loss you have sustained.

A true wife and a devoted mother, no higher eulogy can be pronounced upon any woman. Truly the great central sun of your household has gone down; and I most truly, deeply sympathize with you in your great affliction.

———

1832 Thirteenth Street, N. W.,

Washington, May 9, 1893.

From Thomas Y. Yeates, Secretary of

St. George's North American Union:

I have this A. M. been informed by Brother Underdown of your great loss, and I hasten to tender the sympathies of a husband who has a noble, faithful and loving wife, and who can therefore, to some extent, appreciate what the loss of such a wife as yours is to you.

Romaine, Baltimore, May 9, 1893.

From Hon. Edgar G. Miller:

I cannot refrain from writing a little word to you. The sad intelligence reaches us to-day of the departure of your companion and our friend. Her poor health and weakness of frame must have led you to the consciousness of this coming; but the blow falls heavily, not only upon her beloved family, but upon all with whom she was associated. She was so gentle, yet so energetic; so intelligent, so kind, so untiring. Her monument is already raised in her good works, and in her admirable family around you still. May you and they be comforted by the thought of her attained peace, and the loving memory in which she will be held by so many.

———

Shawmont, Philadelphia, May 9, 1893.

From Mrs. Cora Shaw Wilson:

From the depths of my heart I feel a daughter's sympathy and affection for you in the heavy sorrow that has fallen upon you.

I have felt the weight of the " Cross," and know how the heart cries out against the hand of death; but above and beyond it all, like a star,

has risen the ascension, the glorious promises of "The Christ" and the hope of Heaven, and I am comforted.

May you feel the loving consolation of the Saviour who is ever with us all, in the sunshine and shadows of life.

Surely in all the realms of Heaven there can be no more beautiful spirit than Mrs. Lucas. Womanhood has been elevated by her charity, tenderness and godliness of purpose.

Well may we wonder how it is that such an one should be taken; but Heaven hath her needs as well as earth, and thus it is that the flowers of earth to-day become the flowers of Heaven to-morrow.

———

Shawmont, Philadelphia, May 9, 1893.
From Joseph Wilson :

The true, gentle, womanly Mrs. Lucas has gone beyond the low-hanging white clouds, and the high blue dome above; but a fragrance like the odor of the white violet pervades the memory of that "Sister of Mercy" to mankind, and though no sympathy of mine can alleviate your suffering, yet I would have you know at this period that my eyes are wet with yours,

that her lovely form stands before me magnified and glorified with the sanctity of the life I loved to quote as the exemplification of an unselfish, loving mother. May God bless the memory of such a mother—I say this as a son.

———

Camden, N. J., May 10, 1893.
From George F. Fort, Esq.:

In common with your host of friends, sympathizing with you just now, let me also send my line of sorrows for the loss of your wife—a calamity so great, that no words are equal to expressing it.

I had always looked upon your household as a typical one, and where such thorough sympathetic affection existed as between yourself and Mrs. Lucas it would be impossible to imagine one more so.

———

Washington, May 11, 1893.
From Charles F. Benjamin, Esq.:

You have the true sympathy of friends and fellow-countrymen here for the loss that has come upon you and your household, and there are some of us that cannot soon forget the gracious one from whom you are parted for a time.

New York, May 11, 1893.

From John F. Carmon:

I know that this letter will find you filled with grief at the loss of your dear wife. You have indeed suffered a great affliction; a more faithful partner never lived, and few men, I venture to say, ever enjoyed more domestic tranquillity than yourself. "A true wife and a devoted mother;" no higher eulogy can be pronounced upon any woman. Truly the great central sun of your household has gone down, and I most truly, deeply sympathize with you and yours in your affliction. I deeply realize that expressions of condolence wholly fail to restore the loved and lost one, yet I cannot but hope that the heartfelt sympathy of a sincere friend will not be deemed intrusion on your grief.

———

May 12, 1893.

From Mrs. Julia Trenwith:

I do not think there is any one who can sympathize more with you than we can in your very severe loss of your noble and good wife. Oh, how sad it is to give up our loved ones! But we must bow with submission to our Holy Father, and say, "Thy will be done." I have a

33

precious legacy from Mrs. Lucas, in a beautiful letter which she wrote to us while in bed, and I shall always treasure it.

———

18 Hopper Street, Utica, N. Y.,
May 12, 1893.

From Daniel Batchelor, Esq. :

A letter from Mr. Underdown, received on the ninth instant, brought me the sad news of your bereavement. I know well enough that without my using the conventional words of condolence, you will believe me when I say I deeply sympathize with you in your great affliction. More than thirty years ago I lost a dear wife and have since then been afflicted many times by the loss of daughters, son, sisters, brothers, and last month a dear grand-daughter in her nineteenth year. Dear John, it is an adage that "the penalty of longevity is that our friends die away from us." I think that it is one of the penalties of living at all.

Yesterday's mail brought me a letter in your own handwriting, and enclosing a copy of most tenderly pathetic verses, composed by you, for your dear one, dated December 16, 1892. There is an exquisitely natural pathos in your lines and

most admirably expressed. I have read them to my wife who said on hearing them, "How sacred that poem must be to Mr. Lucas now."

"But if the Spring, ah! if the Spring led on to Summer." Let it not be doubted but that the Spring led your dear one on to the eternal Summer of everlasting bliss.

May the blessings of Heaven come to you in the sweet remembrance of the dear departed.

---

Olean, N. Y., May 12, 1893.
From Rev. J. W. Ashton :

I have been unable to write while feeling the pangs of grief which dear Mrs. Lucas' death has occasioned. And now, although all is over, as it were, I cannot convey any idea of my sense of personal loss, or the deep sympathy that I feel for you and the dear bereaved family.

I can only say, she was a woman of unquestioning faith and unbounded love, and will be missed more and more as years roll on. Such love, such friendship, such heroic devotion to what she deemed her duty, has rarely been equalled, never surpassed.

It was impossible, of course, for me, under the circumstances, to attend the funeral, and I did

not encourage Mrs. Ashton's going for similar reasons. It is a comfort to have been with her a few times before she passed away, as it was her wish that I should be, and in any way to have ministered to her happiness. Her memory is cherished, as she was one of our dearest and truest friends.

———

St. Louis, May 12, 1893.

From T. M. Page, Esq.:

I have this moment seen a notice of your bereavement, and am moved to write to you by recollection of your last interview with my father, in November, 1891. He lived until the following February, and often told me how glad he was to have seen you once more on earth.

It is in times of sorrow that men feel the need of honest sympathy of their fellow-men. I know that lesson by heart. For three years it has been brought home to me. In that time I have lost both father and mother, and now, an only child, unmarried, I am living alone in the old home.

Fortunately, you have children to lighten your loss by sharing it with you. But at your time

of life such separation is hard for mortal strength to bear.

That the love yet left to you may give you precious cheer is the wish of

T. M. Page.

---

1329 South Broad Street,

May 13, 1893.

John Lucas, Esq. :

Dear Friend : I felt the deepest regret at the announcement of the death of Mrs. Lucas, and I feel it my duty to prepare a memorial of her singularly great and honorable public services, for publication both in the journals, probably the "Press," and in permanent form for presveration.

Her purposes were so much above the usual objects and ambitions of even the best of those who engage in the public service, that she commanded the respect and secured the action of the highest authorities in whatever she proposed. I was very much struck with this fact, when she visited Washington to obtain an appropriation in the aid of silk culture, and I am quite sure that no other person could, and certainly no other person ever did, exercise an equal influence in such a case.

It is a great misfortune that her health and life could not have been spared to continue the direction of women's interest in the World's Fair at Chicago ; she would have honored Pennsylvania, and the whole country indeed, much beyond what I fear will be the result now.

I have had such especial opportunity to participate in Mrs. Lucas' efforts in the public service that I think it my first duty to prepare the memorial I have here referred to. I shall be glad to know if you have any wishes or suggestions in regard to it, and to conform to them in whatever I do.

Very truly and respectfully,

Lorin Blodget.

———

Clifton Springs, N. Y., May 15, 1892.

From Henry Foster, M. D. :

It is with great sorrow that we have heard that Mrs. Lucas has left you, and we hasten to express to you, and to your family, the sincere sympathy of Mrs. Foster and myself in this great bereavement.

Mrs. Lucas seemed so frail last autumn, that we feared the result of the great responsibilities which she was carrying ; but her indomitable

will seemed to rise above her physical condition, and we hoped she might be enabled to complete her work.

May God help you all to bear this sorrow, and comfort your hearts in this time of trouble. Mrs. Foster joins me in the expression of our sympathy, and the assurance of our regard.

———

Louisville, Ky., May 13, 1893.
From J. R. Goldsborough :

I have just read in a letter from the office the sad notice of your recent lamentable bereavement, and while I know that the tenderest expressions of sympathy and condolence can do but little to assuage the deep grief that must come with such dispensations, the heart promptings of one who has been befriended, not only by the living, but by the loved one gone to her reward, cause me to proffer to you in your sorrow the sincere sympathy and sorrow I feel for you, and which is extended with equal feeling to all the members of your bereaved and sorrow-stricken household.

Clifton Springs, N. Y., May 15, 1893.
From Bradford Loveland, M. D.:

I was much pained to learn, as I did only a few days since, of your very sad bereavement, and my heart has gone out toward you in your affliction.

Few men could have such a bereavement, for few men have such a wife to lose.

But I suppose we must look to "Him who knoweth all things, and never afflicts willingly the children of men," and in Him and from Him, get the strength and patience to bear what he puts on us.

The remembrance of her life will be to you as the last sweet fragrance of roses that though fallen, bless the air about them, till you go to meet her where there is no sickness, no parting and no death.

You may feel assured that you have the heartfelt sympathy of all your friends and acquaintances here.

———

Philadelphia, May 14, 1893.
From Henry E. Dwight, M.D.:

I thank you for the kind remembrance of our household in the mourning card received

yesterday. For thirty years, ever since my return from Europe at the completion of certain studies incidental to professional life, I have had the privilege of knowing yourself and wife. To me it has been a great privilege, both in social life and in our common duties as citizens, to observe her remarkable ability, fitness and grace in every circle of society in which she moved—in Church and State, among the rich, in the higher walks, among the poor in their poverty, she was always the same dignified, intelligent, eminently attractive and useful woman.

To have trained such a family from infancy to adult years, is more than most women accomplish in life ; to have been the guiding mind, not in female circles only, nor in one church merely, nor in beneficial societies simply, but over and above all these, to be recognized as a social leader in our best society, in all forms of activity, in organizations, which begin with the cradle, and follow the poor, the sick, and the helpless to the grave, is to be a queen among women, wearing a coronet of the highest rank, honored and beloved by all mankind.

Such, my dear friend, was your beloved partner in life. We all share with you this loss, for we all have lost a friend, a partner in our common work, as citizens, as parents, as churchmen, in our families, and our beloved city.

This is the Lord's day, fit time for reflection, for sympathy with those in sorrow and distress. I would say more, but at the remembrance of thirty long years of such usefulness for God and humanity, the record speaks for itself. It needs no eulogy. With the tenderest sympathy for yourself and family,

Henry E. Dwight.

———

Roanoke, Va., May 14, 1893.

Messrs. John Lucas & Co.,
Philadelphia, Pa.

Gentlemen : Yours of the 9th inst. at hand. I am very sorry to hear of Mr. Lucas' sad bereavement in the death of his wife. I never had the pleasure of meeting Mrs. Lucas, but have heard much of her many noble and charitable acts and Christian virtues. My friend, Hugh McIlheny, of Staunton, Va., told me of a reception she gave him and a committee of gentlemen sent to Philadelphia from

Virginia, on some charitable mission, and how pleasant and gracefully she received them, with a beautiful and appropriate address.

From all that I have heard of her she must have been a very superior woman. Please extend my sympathy and regards to Mr. Lucas.

Very respectfully,

J. M. Westmoreland.

———

Letter sent by the firm of John Lucas & Co. to its representatives :

Philadelphia, May 9, 1893.

We regret to announce the decease, on the eighth instant, of Mrs. Harriet A. Lucas, wife of Mr. John Lucas.

Mrs. Lucas had been quite unwell for nearly two years, but it was only within the last few months, that her indomitable energy would succumb to the feebleness of the body. Notwithstanding the enforced confinement to her room, she, by means of a secretary, carried on the work assigned her, as a Commissioner of the World's Fair from Pennsylvania, also her interest in the Woman's Silk Culture Association (with which she was so long

identified) and other public and private charities. Her last appearance in public, was as presiding officer at a meeting of the Pennsylvania Commissioners, and in a reception tendered its members by herself. Although suffering intensely, she went from her room, successfully carried out the programme, and returned never to leave home again.

There was hardly a cause needing help but what Mrs. Lucas came to the front with assistance, both in time and means. The energy displayed in sustaining the almost innumerable charitable interests, public-spirited endeavors, and private benevolences, with which she was connected, doubtless overtaxed the hitherto vigorous constitution, until now the working time is over, and she rests from her self-sacrificing labors.

To Mr. John Lucas, who has been confined to his house for nearly a year, the separation is most sad and painful, while the sons and daughters have lost one of the kindest and most devoted of mothers.

Yours truly,

John Lucas & Co.

3809 Chestnut Street,

May 15, 1893.

From John Sparhawk, Esq. :

Not having seen you when I called at your house, last week, I wish to avail myself of this opportunity of saying how deep and earnest has been the sympathy we all have felt for you and yours in this your season of great bereavement. The removal of your dear wife, however, is not a loss confined to your own immediate home-circle. It is a sorrow which comes to take its place at innumerable firesides, which have been made brighter by her life and influence. It is a loss to her city and her race.

I shall never forget the days we all spent together in the South,—her sunshine and her cheer. I especially recall her kindly words to the widow of the man who was accidentally killed in the changing of the gauge in North Carolina. It was only a part of that abundant charity which "thinketh no evil, and which seeketh not its own."

Undoubtedly the days of her years have been shortened by the ministrations which spent her strength and drained her vital energies. From

labors such as these she falls asleep, and through the great silence passes on "to where beyond these voices there is peace."

———

Clifton Springs, N. Y.,

May 16, 1893.

From Mrs. Alice F. Tatum:

My thoughts have often turned to you and your family in the last few days, since I heard of the great sorrow that has come to you,—a trial so great, that I felt it was beyond the power of words or human sympathy to reach. I don't know any one of whom it could be so fitly said, "None knew her but to love her, none named her but to praise." I do thank you very much for sending me the verses, which reached me yesterday; they are very lovely, and I prize them highly. There have been many expressions of kind feelings and sympathy for you from the various officers of this household, and from the servants who waited upon both of you. Dr. Loveland intends writing to you, and Dr. Foster would, I am sure, send a special message, if he knew I was writing.

Washington, May 17, 1893.

Hon. John Lucas :

Dear Friend : Just received notice that your good wife had passed to her reward. The good works and lovely Christian example she has perfumed this earth with, will live after her, and in imperishable characters. It is inscribed on the hearts of all that knew her. Why such good women should be taken, and those left who but cumber the ground, is beyond my ken. I do know the world is better that Mrs. Lucas lived in it.

It must be a comforting solace, that the good deeds done by your dear wife, will also rise up to call her blessed and be a benediction to you.

Yours truly,

W. W. Dudley.

———

Philadelphia, May 17, 1893.

My Dear Mr. Lucas :

I am gratified by your kind thoughtfulness in sending me the affectionate remembrance card of one who was so active and devoted to all good, benevolent and patriotic work.

In the death of your beloved wife Philadelphia and the country at large has been deprived of the inestimable services of one who was eminent in her zeal and activity in matters of

47

common weal, as well as in active Christian benevolence. Her place cannot be supplied. I am sure I feel and express but the general sentiment. Permit me to express also my deep sympathy, both to you and those around you, in your deep affliction, and believe me,

Very truly yours,

Edward Shippen.

---

1316 Spruce Street, Philadelphia,

May 18, 1893.

From Robert C. Ogden, Esq.:

In common with your large circle of friends and the entire community, myself and family have been mourning with you and yours the loss of Mrs. Lucas. I have no theory upon which to explain the mystery of sorrow, and can only, out of an experience of bereavement, tender you the poor comfort of my sympathy, in this period of darkness and loss.

Sincerely yours,

Robert C. Ogden.

---

Chicago, May 19, 1893.

Dear Mr. Lucas:

I was much pained in taking up a paper here, of last week, to read of the death of your

good wife. I must send just a line to express my sympathy in this great trial.

I thought of her the other day as I was in the Fair Grounds, looking at some of the springing flowers. I saw one named "Director Lucas." Her influence was no doubt greatly felt in this greatest of the World's Fairs.

I think much of her and her hard faithful work for our Home of Rest, and know that we are much indebted to her for faithful service at a time when it must have been a great strain upon her health. With sincerest sympathy, I remain,

Yours very truly,

Robert A. Edwards,
Rector of Church of St. Matthias,
Philadelphia.

———

Kingston, Ont., May 19, 1893.

Dear Sir and Brother:

I am in receipt to-day of the mourning card in memory of your late and excellent wife, Harriet Anne Lucas. Her death came with terrible force. I had always anticipated the pleasure of entertaining her here whenever the Convention should be held in this city.

It was one of the greatest pleasures I looked forward to. On behalf of the Brethren I beg to tender you and the members of your family our heartiest sympathy and condolence at the irreparable loss you have sustained.

With kind regards, I am,

Yours, fraternally,

A. W. Smythe,

President St. George's Union.

———

Springfield, Eden Bridge,

Kent, England, May 20, 1893.

Dear Mr. Lucas:

On opening the envelope just received from you I was saddened and startled to see the news of the great bereavement which has fallen upon you by the loss of your wife, whom to know was to respect and admire. For the bright spirit which has passed away, and now pursues her upward and onward course in a fuller and freer life, we need not grieve, but for those she has left behind, and upon whose lives her beneficent light was cast, my sympathy flows out, and I would beg them never to think for one moment that her life has passed from their reach, but to believe that

that self-sacrificing, sympathetic and enthusiastic spirit, which once tenanted that mortal frame, is still with them, for God's children in Heaven and God's children on earth are both in their Father's arms, the only difference being that the former may be able to see the Father's face more clearly than the latter.

Fraternally would I grasp your hand in this dark period of your life and express my sympathy with you, and that God will comfort you and yours, as He only can, while you learn this hard lesson of submission, is the belief of your sincere friend,

Edward B. Gilburt.

---

Carlton Club, London, May 20, 1893.
My Dear Mr. Lucas :

I received yesterday the papers with the very sad intelligence of Mrs. Lucas' death, and I hasten to offer you my heartfelt condolence. I sympathize with you sincerely in your heavy affliction. I well know how you must feel, and I will not attempt to write at length at such a time.

Remembering always your courtesies and kindness to me, and regretting that there is

nothing that I can say or do that will lessen your great grief, I am,

Yours sincerely,

(Sir) John H. Puleston.

———

34 Redcliffe Gardens, South Kensington,
May 20, 1893.

My Dear Uncle John:

I cannot tell you how inexpressibly grieved I was to find from the paper I received from you to-day of the terrible blow you have received in losing your dear wife on the eighth of this month. No words of mine can possibly convey comfort to your bereaved heart. I can but pray that the Great Comforter will be with you Himself. May He teach you to say, as dear old George Herbert says,

" Yet take Thy way ; for sure Thy way is best."

I know by bitter experience the awful blank in one's life, when a dearly-loved one is taken from us, and how hard it is to look up through our tears and say, " Thy will be done." For her I know you will rejoice that after the months of weary suffering she is at peace and happy forever. Many will miss her active ministry, I know, and the blank in

the home-circle will be inexpressible. Your own health is no doubt suffering greatly from the shock, but I do trust you will soon be strong again.

May He who knew what it was to weep at the grave of a dear friend comfort you all, dear Uncle and Cousins.

With much love and heartfelt sympathy, your loving niece,           Harriet (Lucas).

———

581 Sherbrooke Street, Montreal, Canada.

May 21, 1893.

Dear Mr. Lucas :

My sister, Mrs. Stanley Bagg, has asked me to enclose her card to the family ; and in doing so I desire to send a few lines and unite with your many other friends in expressing our very sincere and deep sympathy in the great and overwhelming sorrow and loss that has come to yourself and once happy home.

As my memory goes back over the many years of our acquaintance, and I recall the invariable courtesy and kindness of yourself and dear Mrs. Lucas, I feel that our friendship was mutual and unfeigned ; and though my absence from Philadelphia has deprived me of

the privilege of often meeting your lovely wife, I have always entertained a very high respect for her gracious accomplishments and Christian character, as exemplified by her interests and efforts in many good works. After a most useful and well-spent life she is now "forever with the Lord."

> "The Saints of God their vigils keep,
> While yet their mortal bodies sleep,
> Till from the dust, they too shall rise
> And soar triumphant to the skies.
> Oh ! happy Saints ; forever blest,
> At Jesus' feet how safe your rest.".

Accept, dear sir, for yourself and all with you, our united kind regards and sympathy, and believe me,

Very faithfully and respectfully,

Fanny M. Mitcheson.

———

30 King's Road, Brighton, England,
May 21, 1893.

My Dear Brother:

We received a newspaper on Friday last, conveying the sad news of dear sister Harriet's death, with great sorrow. We sympathize with you very much in the loss of one with whom you have been treading life's pathway for so many years. To your home circle the

loss must be irreparable, as no one could hear your children speak of her without seeing how tenderly she was loved.

While she was in England last, she won the love of both Alice and myself, and until the last few months we have looked forward to seeing her again in England. Her later letters have breathed such a tone of illness, that we feared the day of parting was not far off; but as years pass on and old age gains upon us all, the time seems not far distant when we, too, shall have joined the growing circle in Heaven.

Let us know how you are, when you have time and feel like writing. We often speak of you, and wonder if you have found relief for your rheumatism. With our love and sympathy to all your family and to yourself,

Believe me, my dear brother,

Affectionately yours,

(Mrs. Edward Lucas) M. Lucas.

---

Tallahassee, Florida, May 21, 1893.

My Dear Mr. Lucas:

Some one has sent me from Philadelphia a card announcing the death of your much-

beloved wife, and my beloved friend. It is a long time since I heard either from or of her, though I wrote often to inquire, and I feared that either herself or some member of her family was in suffering health, but I was not prepared for such distressing news, which wherever heard will carry sorrow. While I express to you my sincere sympathy I feel that I need consolation myself, as do so many friends. I sincerely believe there never lived a more lovely woman, a more beautiful character. I am too much grieved to even attempt condolence. I see nothing to comfort; her loss is irreparable, and alone in sweet memories can we rest; with me she will always thus live. I wish one of her daughters would write me of her last days. It is a year since I received any communication from her, she was then distressed about the health of her youngest daughter and one son.

Present me most affectionately to your family, and I hope that they and yourself will remember that you have a friend in Florida.

I am, with great esteem, yours truly,

Ellen Call Long.

Highbury Moor,
Birmingham, England, May 27, 1893.
From Hon. Joseph Chamberlain:

Dear Mr. Lucas: I have received with much regret your card announcing the bereavement which you have recently sustained. I beg to recall myself to your recollection, and to assure you of my sincere sympathy in your affliction. Believe me to be,

Yours very truly,

J. Chamberlain.

———

Philadelphia, May 24, 1893.
Mr. John Lucas:

My Dear Friend: Although some little time has elapsed since I heard of the death of your wife, I have not been unmindful of you, and desire to be permitted to add my poor tribute to the hosts of your friends, and to say how sincerely I sympathize with you and your family in your irreparable loss.

I had not the privilege and pleasure to be much acquainted with Mrs. Lucas, but have met her within the past few years two or three times. But I knew of her, and of many of her good works, and in common

with the entire community, entertained for her a very high regard and admiration.

To you and her children she was a precious wife and mother—a gift from God. He gave and He hath taken. The work on earth completed, He called her home to be forever with Him in that blessed abode prepared for those who have faithfully loved and served Him.

> Sincerely your friend,
> Robert J. Shoemaker.

———

> 74 Chatham Street, Liverpool,
> May 24, 1893.

Dear Mr. Lucas :

Mrs. R. Wilson has sent me a Philadelphia paper containing the notice of dear Mrs. Lucas' death. In April she wrote me a most affectionate letter, telling me of her very serious illness. On the 13th of May I received from her a pamphlet and her photograph, which I shall greatly treasure ; and though knowing her to be seriously ill, I had hoped she would recover, but it has pleased our Heavenly Father to call her to her well earned rest. To you and her large family it

is a sad loss, and it is difficult to find words to express my grief and sympathy in such a time of sorrow. How blessed the memory must be of such a devoted well-spent life, though comparatively short. We had indulged the hope of her paying us another visit to "Kirkby," where amidst its quiet surroundings she would have regained health.

I hope your own health is much better than when your late dear wife wrote to me. With deepest sympathy and kind remembrance, believe me to be,

Very sincerely yours,

Catharine E. Slack.

———

Kirkby-on-Bain, Horncastle, England,

May 24, 1893.

Dear Mr. Lucas:

I feel quite inadequate to express to yourself and family my grief and sympathy for the loss of so good a wife and mother. It is only eight days since I received her last token of remembrance and kindness to me and little Robbie; a short time previous Mrs. Slack sent me a letter she had received from your dear wife. We were both grieved

to note how very ill and weak she was. Often have we expressed a wish that we could have further opportunities of spending quiet times together in my little home. She must have been a hard worker, and now she will be enjoying the rest of her faithful stewardship.

Hoping yourself and family will be sustained in this sad trial, and with affectionate sympathy, I remain,

Very sincerely yours,

M. Wilson.

———

Green Bank House, Birkdale,
near Liverpool, England,
May 27, 1893.

From William Gibson, Esq.:

My Dear Sir: The receipt of your remembrance card, also of newspaper conveying the melancholy information of the death of your good wife, caused me much and sincere regret. I remember so well her kindly treatment to myself when a stranger and in a strange land, and her conversation as regards your numerous offspring made me look upon her as a truly good wife, and mother. And I need not say that most sincerely do I sympathize with you

under this great trial and bereavement and offer my condolence under it. Young in years, comparatively, I did not expect to hear of her being so early called away from a life in which she has been of so much use to so many of her fellow creatures. A life so spent that it must leave to you naught but pleasing reflections in your old age.

———

Vancouver, B. C., May 25, 1893.

My Dear Mr. Lucas :

It is with great sorrow that I learn from a letter received from Mrs. Mason of the mournful bereavement you have been called upon to suffer in the loss of your dear wife.

Such a wife and such a mother are not often met with, and far beyond her own family circle the many estimable qualities of heart and mind of which Mrs. Lucas was the happy possessor endeared her to all who had the privilege to know her.

Being away out on the Pacific Coast I have only just heard of the sad event, but I assure you I feel it as a personal loss, and tender you my most heartfelt condolence in this the time of your tribulation.

Having passed through a similar ordeal myself, I can the more readily enter into your feelings and sympathize with you in your loneliness and grief, and I pray that you and Miss Lucas may be sustained and consoled by Him who alone can comfort the mourner, who is too wise to err, and too good to be unkind, and whose every act and purpose we must believe to be prompted by love.

Knowing how little human help or sympathy can avail in assuaging sorrow such as yours, I can only assure you of my deep sympathy, in which I am sure my wife joins, and with our very kind regards to yourself and Miss Lucas I remain,

Faithfully yours,

J. Herbert Mason.

——

The Old Hall, Stone, Staffordshire, England,
May 26, 1893.

From Miss Annie Masfield:

We were indeed very sorry to hear of the very sad loss you have had, and we all beg you will accept our very sincere sympathy. We see from the card you sent that Mrs. Lucas died on the eighth of this month, the same day on which

our dear mother passed away, thirteen years since.

We can quite understand how very much Mrs. Lucas will be missed, not only by her own family-circle, but by all who knew her. Hers was a very valuable and useful life.

———

Philadelphia, May 30, 1893.
From W. Waterall :

My Dear Old Friend: I have purposely deferred writing you an expression of sympathy in your bereavement until I could more review the closing of an important chapter in my own life's experience, and a sorrow that must move your life to its innermost depths. The light that has just gone out has been visible on the pathway of my life's pilgrimage for thirty-five years. My thoughts in tender memories instinctively turn towards those earlier years of our friendship, when the light of that intelligence cheered and heightened all things in "The home by the Lake and the Wood." Especially when she, with her gifted mother, gave pure and lofty tone to the intellectual atmosphere that ever pervaded the walks in the dear old woods, and the talks by

the Lake and fire-side. I shall always love best to think of Harriet as the charming young wife and mother, making that country home attractive and beautiful, surrounded by her interesting young family, whose tender minds she would continually impress with her own intense love for the English Church.

Permit me in all sincerity to express the hope that both you and your dear children may do all that you can to strengthen and perpetuate the life of "St. John in the Wilderness," and thus make it the most appropriate and enduring memorial of one who devoted so much loving energy in planting and stimulating its early growth.

Trusting that kind Heaven will deal gently with you in your two-fold affliction,

I am, sincerely your friend,

W. Waterall.

Mr. John Lucas.

———

4400 Spruce Street, May 31, 1893.
From Mary E. Ashman.

Mr. Dear Mr. Lucas: The thoughtful remembrance in sending the Memorial card of your dear wife is most gratefully appreciated

by both Mr. Ashman and myself. I mentioned to your daughter Bessie, at the " Boys' Temporary Home," a short time before Mrs. Lucas went to her other home, how sorry both Mr. Ashman and I were to hear of her severe illness, and also to say how much Mr. Ashman always admired her as a woman, her sprightliness and ability. She certainly was a remarkable woman—one that you will miss every hour of your life, and that the kindest attention of your children cannot replace.

Please accept our warmest sympathy. I hope your health is improved.

With kind regards, I am,

Very respectfully,

Mary E. Ashman.

———

132 Longacre, London, England,

June 6, 1893.

From George Slatter, Esq. :

On my return to London, after a continental trip, I found the newspaper announcing your sad bereavement. I look back to remember the short time I was in your company, when Mrs. Lucas was with you here. She seemed to

have high intellectual gifts and boundless impulses towards every good work; and who shall number the people whose lives have been made better and prospects brighter by her influence and grand endeavors. Think what the world would be if a small percentage of the people we live amongst had such a record. Will you please express to your kind family my most ample sympathy and condolence.

(Mr. Slatter was a personal friend of the late Honorable John Welsh.)

———

Philadelphia, June 7, 1893.

John Lucas, Esq.

Dear Sir: The ladies of the Tenth Ward Charity Organization desire me to communicate to you their sympathy and sorrow for the loss of your beloved wife, the much honored President of our Association.

She was with us from the beginning, nearly twenty years ago.

She was very highly esteemed for her unusual business capacity and great generosity, and also for her untiring willingness to assist in every call for aid.

Her loss to us is a very serious one, and we heartily sympathize with you in your and our bereavement.

> Very respectfully yours,
>> Frances Cooper,
>>> Secretary.

———

Junior Athenæum Club, 116, Piccadilly, W.,
> London, England, June 7, 1893.

My Dear Mr. Lucas:

It was with feelings of deep distress I received the very sad news of the death of your greatly respected and much loved wife.

Allow me, in all sincerity, to offer you and your family-circle, my heartfelt sympathies in this the day of your great trouble, and to hope and believe that your loss is her eternal gain. With every good wish, believe me,

> Sincerely yours,
>> James T. Turnbull.

———

> Chicago, June 10, 1893.

From Mrs. E. W. Allen:
> World's Fair Commission:

Dear Mr. Lucas: You have probably long since been informed that your telegram to our

President, Mrs. Palmer, announcing the death of your dear wife was read in the meeting of the Executive Committee. We were all profoundly impressed with a sense of our great loss, and sympathize with you most deeply in your bereavement, realizing, as we do, that one of the most able and earnest members of our Board will be no longer with us in our work on earth, and that there must be a great blank in the home from which such an one has departed.

In the midst of our mourning, however, let us remember that she has gone to a better home, where there will be no more pain, and where we may meet her again with no thought of parting. Though we linger yet a little longer she has already heard the welcome greeting : " Well done, good and faithful servant, enter thou into the joy of thy Lord."

Whether the gates of the World's Fair are open on the Lord's day or not, let us rejoice that she was permitted to utter her protest in words which were no less firm than gentle.

In deepest sympathy,

Mrs. E. W. Allen.

1313 Somerset Street, Philadelphia,
June 19, 1890.

From Robert Watchorn, Esq.:

This is a very late date on which to express one's sympathy for you in a great bereavement, but I assure you that my sympathy and sorrow is none the less sincere and profound on that account, for ever since I learned that Mrs. Lucas was dead I have been constantly thinking of you and yours, and my heart has been very sad for you all.

Mrs. Lucas was always very kind to me, and took a deep interest in the work of my department, and I feel a personal loss in her departure. I have read the poems of her mother (book which you kindly gave me), and when I recall that the authoress was born in the same grand old historic town as I, it furnishes another cause for my interest in her memory.

———

West Jersey Press, Camden, June 20, 1893.
Mr. John Lucas:

Dear Sir: The world can never know the great loss you have sustained in the death of your estimable wife. But it will in a measure

feel that in her departure humanity is deprived of one who lost no opportunity to show that her thoughts were ever alert in its behalf.

Your truly,

S. Chew.

————

1520 Spruce Street, Philadelphia,
June 23, 1893.

My Dear Mr. Lucas:

I regret exceedingly that absence from the city will prevent my being present at the services to be held in memory of your dear wife at Gibbsboro on to-morrow.

I should feel it a duty to pay this last tribute of respect to the memory of one who in life, though afflicted with sickness, was ever extending a helping hand to the needy and sorrowing, no matter how lowly their condition, or what their race or color.

I recall with much satisfaction the delightful conversation I had with her two years ago at Atlantic City, in regard to the distressed and downfallen, and though she has left us, her memory will be ever held in loving remembrance by her friends, and the many she has aided by her benevolence.

Trusting that you are in the enjoyment of health, I remain,

Ever cordially your friend,

Ferdinand J. Dreer.

———

Chicago, June 29, 1893.

Mr. John Lucas

My Dear Sir: Your invitation to the services in remembrance of Mrs. Lucas has just been received. We have a monument here in her memory, you know, in the beautiful Silk Exhibit. I looked upon this as a dying request, and aside from the fact that I believed in it, I was determined upon that account to see it through to the successful termination, and you will all be glad to know that it is more than a success,—a vast crowd of people around it all the time. Miss Ford tells me that while watching the interest of the people in it, she would give anything to have dear Mrs. Lucas there for just five minutes; but, after all, maybe she was there— who knows? We take great pleasure in the thought.

I think that you and your daughters all should come out to the Fair. It is an educa-

tion that you could not afford to miss, and the dear wife and mother took such deep interest in it that you could look upon it as part of her work. When you come please let me know, as I shall want to see you all.

Yours truly,

A. B. Farquhar,

Executive Commissioner.

———

Chicago, June 30, 1893.

Dear Mr. Lucas :

While passing through the great White City I came across the exhibit of the Women's Silk Culture Association. I stood still for a moment, a mist clouded my eyes, and in the midst of the throbbing multitude of people my tears fell fast and unchecked. Before me stood the monument—the silk flags, the loom, the reels, the cocoons—while beside me I seemed to feel the spirit of the founder, the promoter, the noble, earnest, beloved Mrs. John Lucas. I do not write to open the wounds (for they can never close) but to tell you that the whole atmosphere of the exhibit is hers, hers only, and must ever remain so. In her memory I bought a little souvenir

of the exhibit, and brought away several copies of the tribute to her noble worth—one of which I enclose, and with kindest regards to yourself and the members of your family, I am.

Always yours, most gratefully,

Joseph R. Wilson.

———

Philadelphia, July 20, 1893.

Mr. John Lucas :

My Dear Sir : I regret that my absence in Chicago, on the 24th of June, deprived me of the opportunity of attending the Memorial services in the "Little Church in the Wilderness," of which Mrs. Lucas spoke with so much interest and affection.

I have read the interesting address on that occasion, and it does no more than justice to one of the noblest women of the age ; and her work and example have done much to bring the women of these closing years of the Nineteenth Century to the front in all the departments of active industry.

You and your family have my deepest sympathy in your affliction, and it may be a pleasant thought when you remember that the

world is better because Mrs. Harriet Anne Lucas lived in it.    Yours truly,

John W. Woodside.

Commissioner.

———

All Saints' School,

Germantown, Philadelphia, May 9, 1893.

From Sister Mary Raphael of All Saints:

When I was told of dear Mrs. Lucas' death this morning my heart went out to you with so great a sympathy, I felt I must write and let you know how I felt for you and yours. I know, too, what Carrie would have thought and done, and I know you will miss her doubly at this time; but you have many loving sympathizers in your own children, and Carrie will help you in some special way, even now.

You must not let this heavy trial weigh you down too much, for your children will have more need than ever of you now.

———

Philadelphia, May 11, 1893.

Mr. John Lucas and family:

At a meeting of the Executive Board of the Woman's Homœopathic Association, held this

day, the announcement of Mrs. Lucas' death being made, the Secretary was instructed to send to you an expression of sympathy.

Mrs. Lucas was with us from the inception of our work as an Association, and has always shown the deepest interest in its objects.

Although for the past year or more, on account of failing health and manifold duties, she was unable to take so active a part as formerly in our affairs. Even so late as a few weeks ago she showed practically her interest by collecting and sending to our Treasurer the money from her annual subscribers.

A personal friend to many of us, and to all of us dear through mutual interest and coöperation, she will long be missed, and it is not a formal, but a heartfelt sympathy that we extend to you in your great bereavement.

For the Board:

Fanny L. Skinner, Secretary.

———

727 Walnut Street, May 11, 1893.

My Dear Mr. Lucas:

At our meeting yesterday, as you may well believe, the sad loss you have sustained in

the death of your excellent wife was upper-most in every mind. And they endeavored feebly to express their own sorrow, and their desire to join with you, and the members of the family, in their appreciation of the sad bereavement. The resolutions which I enclose, in some degree express those feelings; but over and above all that language can express, let each of us say, that we sincerely condole with you, and with them.

Sincerely yours,

W. T. Pratt.

The Hayes Mechanics' Home,

Philadelphia, May 11, 1893.

The Managers of the Hayes Mechanics' Home have to record upon their minutes with affectionate remembrance the death of Mrs. Harriet A. Lucas, wife of John Lucas, which occurred on the morning of Monday, May 8.

The deceased was active in the organization of this Home, became one of the Managers and subsequently Vice-President, and during the years that have passed evinced the most earnest interest in its welfare, in words, as well as by active attention to its administration.

Endowed with admirable executive ability and possessing that warmth of heart that caused her to become interested in many institutions that were devoted to charity, or the good of humanity in any form, she was yet able to give a portion of her valuable time to the advancement of this Home; and we record our heartfelt appreciation of those services in its cause, with our personal grief that we shall not again meet her kindly smile, and that her valued life is so soon brought to a close.

In the death of this estimable lady the cause of humanity has lost one of its most efficient workers, this Institution a devoted advocate, and to us, personally, a kind associate and friend.

W. T. Pratt, Secretary.

———

Woman's Christian Temperance Union,
Philadelphia, May 13, 1893.
To Mr. John Lucas and family :
Dear Sir : At the regular monthly meeting of the W. C. T. U. of Philadelphia, held May 12, 1893, it was unanimously Resolved, that in the death of our Honorary Member, Mrs. John Lucas,

we have lost a valued friend and sympathizer. While Mrs. Lucas' friends are not confined to one city or one State, yet here in the city of her home, where she was best known, and most esteemed for her true benevolence, we realize a keener sense of loss, and desire as a "Union" to express to her husband and family our sincere sympathy for them, in this their time of bereavement.

Very sincerely yours,
Adelaide V. Dutton,
Corresponding Secretary.

———

May 18, 1893.

The Teachers of the Chinese Class of the Epiphany, desire to testify to their sense of loss in the removal from earth of their dear friend, Mrs. John Lucas. They feel that they have lost one who was much to each of them personally, and who was a trusted leader, whose whole heart was in the work of the School. Her presence itself was an inspiration to faithfulness in the cause she loved, because it was her Master's work.

Her co-workers in the class desire to tender their warmest sympathy to the husband and

family of their dear friend in this their sad bereavement; and may the Lord, whom she loved, strengthen and help them in their affliction.

———

St. Peter's Rectory, May 19, 1893.
My Dear Mrs. Potter:

Your blessed mother had passed to her rest sometime before I had heard of it. Many times have we spoken of her. Our Home is indebted to her for its success during its infancy. Her zeal, liberality and courage were most remarkable. When we were faint-hearted she was equal to the emergency, and in her generous offerings carried us over the shadow into light again. I have been many times quickened by her zeal and strengthened by her courage. Though her loss to her family must be beyond their comprehension, I can but think of her blessedness in Paradise, waiting for her resurrection, when she shall "behold Him and be satisfied."

Do, dear friends, retain your interest in our Home. It needs constant help, and do, for your mother's sake, and in loving memory, plead for our sustenance.

Will you give to each member of your family my tenderest sympathy. Her vacancy will be keenly felt, and I humbly pray our great God and Father to help us all to be just as ready when our "call cometh."

Yours most sincerely,

Annie J. Rumney.

———

Bullitt Building,

Philadelphia, May 20, 1893.

Mr. John Lucas:

My Dear Sir: Permit me as Secretary of the Trustees of the Italian Mission to enclose to you the original draft of the Minute adopted by the Board a few days since, relative to the great loss so many have sustained in the death of Mrs. John Lucas, and most especially the organization I have the honor to represent.

Truly,

John Marston, Secretary.

———

Minutes adopted by the Board of Trustees of the Italian Episcopal Mission, May 16, 1893:

The removal of one so largely and actively identified with works of benevolence as

Mrs. John Lucas, may well be regarded as a public loss. Her labors of love and sympathy are known throughout the community.

It is rare indeed to find one combining such force of character with a true woman's amiability, and with such untiring activity and zeal directed by a wise judgment and executive ability. She was one of the earliest friends and laborers in the Italian Episcopal Mission, and maintained an interest in it to the last moments of her life.

The Rector and Trustees have placed this Minute on their Records in grateful remembrance of her services, and request their Secretary to convey to Mr. Lucas their deep sympathy in his bereavement.

Rev. M. Zara, Rector.

John E. Baird, Chairman of Trustees.

John P. Rhoads, Treasurer.

Attest: John Marston, Secretary.

———

Atlantic City, May 31, 1893.

Mr. John Lucas:

Dear Sir: I am very sorry you loss the wise ladie, Mrs. Lucas, she stay with God forever. When she live that time and said,

we have to be end, we will stay with God forever. And hope you far away off not be weary and take good care yourself, and look back your children and grand children and you have the best in the world, but we hope her stay on this world longer, and do more good for our Chinaman. When I talk to my friends who know her, they be sad when she gone, so our friend member her forever when she is live every year the scholars remember the Lake Side Park. Now I do not know how the Park is to be. So who do good the name is fame.

Yours sincerely,

Joe James,

Wing, Wah, Lee & Co.

---

Oregon World's Fair Commission,

Terre Haute, Ind., May 23, 1893.

Dear Mr. Lucas:

I have just learned of the death of your dear wife. It gave me great sorrow to my heart. I thought when I met her in the Fall she wouldn't recover, but did not think that it would be so soon as this.

I never met any person with such a short acquaintance that has made such an impression on me as Mrs. Lucas. I know you will miss her more than tongue can tell. I miss her so much in the convention; but I must leave it to Him that doeth all things well. I am afraid to write any more, as words only cut the wound deeper.

I remain, sincerely yours,

Mrs. Mary Payton,

Lady Manager.

———

St. George's Society,

Washington, May 24, 1893.

John Lucas, Esq.:

Dear Sir and Brother: A recent vote of this society has placed upon me the duty of communicating to you the sympathy felt by our members for you and your household at the calling away of the admirable wife and mother, that some of us had opportunity to know and esteem in life, and whose death we lament with you.

It is a gratification to us to believe that the many expressions of those who feel with

you and for you may make your bereavement a little the easier to bear.

I am, dear sir and brother,

Very sincerely yours,

John H. Howlett,

President of the Society.

Attest: Chas. F. Benjamin, Secretary.

———

Philadelphia, May 23, 1893.

Mr. John Lucas:

Dear Sir: The ladies of the Board of Managers of the "House of Rest," Germantown, desire me to convey to you and your bereaved family their heartfelt sympathy. We feel that we have lost a noble and sympathetic friend—one whose life was spent for others.

Very sincerely,

Mrs. James A. Bennett.

Rebecca F. Bennett, Secretary.

———

St. Jude's Rectory, 816 Franklin Street,

June 1, 1893.

My Dear Mr. Lucas:

At the last meeting of the Board of Managers of the House of Rest I was instructed to draw

up a minute in regard to the death of Mrs. Lucas, and forward the same to you. With deep sympathy, believe me,

Very truly yours,

J. R. Moses.

———

Philadelphia, June 1, 1893.

Extract from minutes of Board of Managers of the House of Rest for the Aged. The Secretary was instructed to prepare a minute in regard to the death of Mrs. Lucas. This minute to be sent to the family and to be put upon the minutes.

"This Board desires to express its deep sense of loss in the removal from among us of Mrs. John Lucas. From the beginning of the work, until the time when ill health compelled her to resign the Presidency of the Board of Women Managers, her indefatigable energy contributed in a great measure to the success of the undertaking. With deep appreciation of her faithful and efficient service, the Board desires to express its hearty sympathy with her bereaved family."

J. R. Moses, Secretary.

# Memorial Notices of the Press.

Many generous and instructive notices of the life and services of Mrs. Lucas were given in the public journals of this city, New Jersey and New York, on the occasion of her death.

It would be a grateful task to transcribe these notices in this connection if space permitted. Their strong expressions of personal regard for her singular devotion to works of mercy, were the most prominent feature, and next the ample statements made as to her practical connection with so many institutions. But as the leading events of her practical life are given in the second portion, or historical part of this Memoir, it is not necessary to repeat them here.

Mr. Lucas desires to make grateful acknowledgment of these Memorial notices. The list is so large that it is scarcely practicable to even cite them more definitely in this place.

Newsboys' Home,
251 South Sixth Street, June 6, 1893.
Mr. John Lucas:

Dear Sir: At the last meeting of the Board, on June 2, the following Resolutions were adopted:

The Board of Managers of the Temporary Home for Young Men and Boys have learned with profound sorrow of the death of their honored President, Mrs. John Lucas, which occurred on Monday, May 8. In view of this sad bereavement it is fitting and proper that this Board should give expression to the sense of heartfelt sorrow which this dispensation of Divine Providence has occasioned.

Resolved, That the death of Mrs. Lucas, our President, has caused a vacancy which we deeply mourn, and which has filled our hearts with grief and sadness.

Resolved, That we hereby testify to the rare intelligence, wise counsel and sincere devotion of Mrs. Lucas to the cause of the Master, during the many years of her consecrated life.

Resolved, That the Church of Christ, the Christian community, and the world at large, have sustained an irreparable loss in her transi-

tion from earth to heaven, and from the cross to the crown.

Resolved, That we deeply sympathize with her honored husband, and sons, and daughters in this hour of their severe affliction, with the earnest prayer that their grief-stricken hearts may find comfort and consolation in the "God of all comfort" in this time of their sad bereavement.

Resolved, That this record be entered on our minutes, and that a copy be transmitted to the afflicted family.

Yours very truly,

Russel T. Boswell,

Secretary.

# History of the Principal Services of Mrs. Lucas in Public Affairs.

———

It is essential to a proper memorial to the memory of Mrs. Lucas to review with some definiteness her successful efforts to advance the interests and improve the condition of many classes. Her work was not all that of simple benevolence in the ordinary sense, so much as it was of deliberate and careful plans, far-reaching in their influence, and in most cases alike beneficial to the whole people. It was this breadth of character, joined with her

singular persistence and untiring faithfulness, that constituted her chief
distinction.

I regret that it is not possible to make
this review of her services complete and
exhaustive as it should be made.  Much
has been incidentally stated on these points
by the writers of the letters of condolence
here printed; but there should be some one
acquainted with the exact details of her
works of strict benevolence, as well as one
to do the work I here attempt of citing
her more general efforts to influence public
affairs.  Having at her command a private
fund with which to assist worthy objects,
making no mention of what she did to
others—not even to members of her own
family—all that she did was so unobtrusive
and so absolutely without the usual
blazoning of publicity, that it is difficult

to trace all of her acts or to get back to the beginning in each case.

The following sketch will therefore be a collection of citations and of incidents such as have come under my immediate notice, rather than an assumption to make a complete history.

And I may also say that a greater purpose entertained in the present case is to relieve all her recent work of any doubt as to its practical success, or as to the appreciation in which it was held by her immediate associates. It is too often the case that what is said of a person intending a public service is, that while it was well intended, it required some other hand to make it practically successful. Such was not the case with the works undertaken by her.

It may be said generally that these active works have occupied somewhat

more than twenty years, in a position of much prominence. Undoubtedly they began earlier, and in the singularly interesting account which I find in her own handwriting of the founding of the church at Gibbsboro, an admirable illustration is given of her persistence in purpose often kept in design some years before the complete execution. In this case she says that in 1856, the first of her residence at Gibbsboro, active efforts were undertaken to build up a social and religious influence, and while these were not all she desired, or rather all that they should be, for almost twenty years afterward they were still prosecuted in good faith and were really of much service. This was an alternative residence only, however, her permanent residence being in Philadelphia, and all her more

important works were undertaken and conducted in this city. The history of the founding of the Gibbsboro Church is of so much interest, however, that her manuscript is here printed in full.

With the various societies organized in part by her, for benevolent purposes, she was always in active co-operation, was not merely a member and contributor, but most active in suggesting and the most persistent in enforcing the practical form to all these efforts. This was especially true of those which are the most difficult in themselves, the charities which were new and without the experience of routine which attaches to so many. In this respect, also, some most striking testimonials are afforded in the letters of condolence before given. The Chinese benevolent efforts, and that

with the Italians also, are illustrations of the vigor and success of movements in which she had the leading place. They were all intended to be instructive and beneficial in the most direct degree, and never represented any sectarian feeling, or any propagandism of the views of one church over another. When efforts such as hers are so openly and unselfishly made, all these limits and distinctions break down of themselves.

Perhaps her more active career, from about 1872 to the present year, will represent the more conspicuous of her efforts and services. During this period she was connected with about twenty societies and organizations, in several of which she took the leading part. With enough, as it is usually supposed, of occupations and burdens in her family

relations, there was still no time in which she hesitated or declined to act when she consistently could for the public. She did so as unconsciously and without effort, as might be supposed if she had no other occupation or purpose whatever.

It must be again said that it is impossible to arrange the evidences of this work in strict chronological order, or to give the whole history connected with it as it should be given. The best will be done, however, which is practicable with the papers at hand.

Among the earliest of the efforts of Mrs. Lucas, in acts of what might be called permanent benevolence, was an effort for the establishment of a Retreat for Aged Divines of the Church. The matter is alluded to in a letter to Mrs. Lucas, of February 6, 1879, from

the Hon. John Welsh, then Minister of the United States at London. The letter of Mr. Welsh is before me, acknowledging the receipt of Mrs. Lucas' proposition, and in this letter Mr. Welsh discusses the principles on which such a retreat, or provision rather, for the maintenance of such persons, should be founded. Not having Mrs. Lucas' letter, it can only be said that she voluntarily took the lead in making such provision, whether by a distinct residence or by an arrangement providing for their residence in private families. It appears that Mrs. Lucas selected the location. Mr. Welsh closes his letter with the statement that he trusts that the zeal of those who have taken the subject in hand will be equal to a successful accomplishment.

As a prominent member of the Episcopal Church, Mrs. Lucas participated in most of the conspicuous charities or institutions which Bishop Stevens was so prominent in founding. The "House of Rest for the Aged," in Germantown, is one of several institutions which passed resolutions of sympathy and sent their condolence to Mr. Lucas and family.

Among the many benevolent institutions in which she took an active part may be named the Tenth Ward Charity Organization, established over twenty years ago, the Hayes Mechanics' Home, the Woman's Homœopathic Association, the Italian Episcopal Mission, the Chinese Mission, the House of Rest for the Aged Women of the Episcopal Church, of which she was the first President of the Board of Lady Managers,

in regard to which the following striking tribute of respect is furnished by Mrs. Rumney:

"Our Home is indebted to her for its success during its infancy. Her zeal, liberality and courage were most remarkable. When we were faint-hearted, she was equal to the emergency, and in her generous offerings carried us over the shadow into light again."

These were but a few of the institutions which she made much more than charity, making them, rather, active and creative agencies for the permanent benefit of all connected with them. The tributes of respect and the acknowledgment of services will in many cases be found in the letters of condolence here printed. It would be an appropriate service on the part of some one more directly connected with these establish-

ments than the writer of this paper, to state in full detail the actual work done in each case by her, and the full list of the charities benefited.

We will now revert to another class of institutions and of services in which Mrs. Lucas has in all cases been prominent and in some of which she has had almost the leading place. These are the several exhibitions of art and industry which have had so prominent a place for thirty years past. She took an active part and gave effective service in the work of the Centennial Exhibition of 1876, although as the organizations then existing did not recognize or distinguish women's departments as such, her name does not appear on any Board of Managers. Her activity and influence, however, are gratefully remembered.

Soon after this came the French Exhibition of 1878, which enlisted a good deal of interest on the part of Americans. Next in succession was the Exhibition at Atlanta, in 1880–1, which being an exhibit of cotton and other fibres elicited a good deal of attention from the ladies of the Association, then newly organized for the promotion of Silk Culture and silk manufacture within the United States. Mrs. Lucas was very active in the formation of this Association, and in the production of silk fabrics, then first becoming prominent in the United States. Mrs. Lucas threw her whole spirit into this effort to advance silk culture and to produce silk fabrics during the year 1880, and she had the aid of many prominent citizens: Governor Pollock, Hon. Thomas H. Dudley, Hon. John W.

Forney, and others; also Governor Hoyt, and Hon. Thomas B. Edge, of the State Agricultural Department. So rapid was the advancement of this industry, that it was proposed to make it prominent in the Atlanta Exhibition, and a remarkably conspicuous and successful exhibit of the products of this industry was made there in the later months of 1880 and early in 1881. Very active work was done by the Association during the summer of 1880, and several meetings were held, at which addresses were made, recognizing, on the part of prominent citizens, public officers and manufacturers, the value of their efforts. Mr. William A. Griswold, of the Darby Mills, aided them very much, and introduced silk industry on a large scale in these mills, as did also Hensel & Colladay, whose

mills were in Philadelphia. A large number of mills in Philadelphia took up one or another form of silk industry about this time, and their present product of silk fabrics amounts to many millions of dollars annually.

To show how well the hopes of Mrs. Lucas were justified as to founding the silk industry on an extensive scale here, I may anticipate by saying that now there are one hundred and twenty silk mills in the State of Pennsylvania, about seventy of which are in Philadelphia, and the product of these mills amounts to nearly $70,000,000 annually. While the cultivation of the raw silk has not been so far successful as to compete with the immense imports of cheap raw silk from India and China, yet the silk goods themselves are now made here in more than twice

the quantity of the present importation, while twenty-five years ago the whole requirement of the country was imported.

Exhibits of silk fabrics, raw silk, cocoons and reeling processes were made at several of the county fairs in 1880 and 1883. While this publicity given to the matter invited the location of silk mills in these interior towns, it is to be regretted that but little raw silk is as yet grown in the State. All of the circumstances of the case are favorable to it in the highest degree however.

The report prepared for the New Orleans Exhibition, credits the Woman's Silk Culture Association with having "conducted an important movement in silk growing, which for three years past has given an impetus to the growing of silk as a domestic resource for families in all parts

of the United States, and has distributed trees, eggs and books of instruction, awarding premiums annually for cocoons, and reeling the silk from the cocoons received. From this reeled silk, fine articles of brocade, flag silks, ribbons, etc., have been made for the Association, and have attracted great attention when publicly shown." This statement, written in December, 1884, is a compact, but still inadequate expression of the work then accomplished by the Association.

## Appropriations by Congress.

Various efforts were made by Mrs. Lucas and her friends to obtain the aid of the general government in their work of promoting silk industry. Some aid was afforded in the year 1885, by the Department of Agriculture, some monthly appropriations being given to aid in silk reeling. In 1886, however, after direct efforts made personally by Mrs. Lucas to the Senate and House Committees, an appropriation of $5,000 was got, which was drawn on July 30, 1886.

It was distinctly placed in the hands of the Silk Culture Association, but with

the requirement to report upon the subject to the Department of Agriculture; the first report so made, being for the fiscal year ending June 30, 1887. In 1887 Congress made a second appropriation of $5,000, under the same conditions, which was drawn on July 19 of that year. The expenditure of this sum was reported to the Department as for the fiscal year ending June 30, 1888.

A third appropriation was made, also of $5,000, which was drawn October 6, 1888. Report upon this expenditure was made for the year ending June 30, 1889. Some conditions were attached to this appropriation, requiring a free distribution of trees and some specific aid to silk growers, but the expenditure in all these cases was chiefly in the payment of cocoons cultivated by experimental growers. In

this last year a considerable sum was also expended in weaving dress and flag silks into fabrics of the highest quality.

A fourth appropriation of $5,000 was made by Congress in 1889, which was drawn upon October 9 of that year. A report upon the expenditure of this sum was made for the fiscal year ending June 30, 1890.

At the end of this year, or on July 1, 1890, about $1,000 remained of the appropriation, and no further appropriation being made, it became necessary to limit the expenditure for trees and the free distribution of articles and directions in aid of silk culture. With its large stock of materials, however, the great confidence of the public in its activity and efficiency continued to fully the end of a second fiscal year, or to July, 1892.

Thus the direct aid of the government was carried over a period of about six years, with a result of carrying on an effective encouragement to this great national industry, at less cost than could have been supposed possible. As only the immediate employés of the Association received salaries, the expenditure for such purposes as usually consume public appropriations was very small indeed. It may safely be said that no such inexpensive and effective public service has been rendered by any official agency, either at Washington or elsewhere.

In recognition of the official relations which they desired to establish, but wholly from their own resources and before any appropriations were made, and in vindication of the effectiveness of their work, the ladies of this Association

prepared sets of magnificent flags, made of silk grown in the United States, reeled in their own rooms in Philadelphia, and woven in our own silk mills. These flags were presented on January 23, 1885, one to the Senate and one to the House of Representatives at Washington, the occasion being made one of the most imposing ceremonial, and the speeches of Senators Beck, Dawes, and Morgan, and of Representative Kelly of the House, being in the highest degree appreciative. These flags were ten by seven feet in size, elaborately furnished and mounted. Resolutions of acceptance were adopted, both by the Senate and House, and are entered at length upon the official records of the Forty-eighth Congress.

Just previous to this presentation, or on January 22, 1885, the Association

presented to the Governor and Legislature of Pennsylvania a stand of two very large National and State flags, made of American silk, reeled, dyed and woven in the City of Philadelphia, which flags were received by Governor Pattison and a joint Committee of the Senate and House, met in the Executive Chamber at Harrisburg. A full report of this presentation was made by the Joint Legislative Committee, on February 26, 1885, and duly recorded in the proceedings of the Legislature.

Other presentations of flags were made about this time, one through Mrs. E. C. Long, of Florida, to the people of that State, on January 6, 1885, which were received by Governor Perry of that State; and it may also be said that handsome flags made by the Association were

presented to the Atlanta Exhibition of 1881.

A schedule is given in the Tenth Annual Report of the Association, of forty-nine distinct exhibits of silk cocoons, reeling, and other processes, as well as finished fabrics of silk made by them in the different States and cities of the United States chiefly, although one was in Mexico, and three were in England. This remarkable schedule can be found at page 21 of the Tenth Annual Report.

A final occasion on which an effective and influential display was made occurred at the meeting of the Pan American Congress, at Washington, in April, 1890. A flag of American silk, spun, woven and finished in the City of Philadelphia, was presented to each delegation from the several States of

South America and Central America, seventeen in number. The replies of the several delegations were appreciative and patriotic in the highest degree.

The design in each of these cases is to be credited to Mrs. Lucas, and her presentation addresses were full of suggestion to the people of the several American States. In closing her address to these South American delegations, she said:

"Gentlemen, bear with you these emblems of the success of our nation, place them in your Legislative halls, and ever regard them as tokens of one hundred years of National prosperity of this Government, of the people, for the people, and by the people, and the devotion of a little band of women to the advancement of home production and industrial education."

# National Exhibitions.

On the general subject of the form in which exhibits are now made of social and industrial progress, it is but just to say that to Mrs. Lucas almost exclusive credit is due for the prominence now held by women's work.

The contrast between the exhibits made at the Centennial, in 1876, with the more complete social and industrial organization of the World's Fair at Chicago, illustrates the statement here made. In the present exhibition there is a recognized department of woman's work, almost equal in

Commission, to take entire charge of the interests of women at the Exposition. This Board has made a most remarkable exhibit, in which educational, artistic and industrial features are almost equally prominent. They have vindicated the claim which American ladies have here first made, that women do possess creative minds, and do constitute the most important factors in the arts of peace and progress as well as in merely charitable and beneficent institutions. They have here shown that they can create new surroundings, new lines of productive work in the most positive sense, and new methods of labor as well as new rewards for labor.

The expenditure by the Directors of $200,000 in the erection of this building has been the most instructive and

significant of the results at Chicago. In the Pennsylvania Book of Instruction and Exhibit this feature is given great prominence, and an admirable statement of the County Societies of Pennsylvania, as well as of the entire plan of collecting and exhibiting there, is given over the signature of Mrs. Lucas, as she was really more than any one else the author of the entire system. This portion of the volume, from page 167 to 187, is worthy to be reprinted and distributed as the most expressive and definite illustration of the gain in woman's position, as well as the elevation of present influences over those prevailing even so recently as the Centennial of 1876.

It should be borne in mind that the Act of Congress creating the National Commission for conducting the World's

Columbian Exposition was passed April 25, 1890, and that this Act gave almost equal prominence as members and managers of said Commission to the Board of Lady Managers, then created. This National Board of Lady Managers consisted of two from each State, and it was incumbent on the Board so created to outline, as far as possible, the work falling to them to do. In this work Mrs. Lucas and her alternate, Miss McCandless, were engaged for more than a year before the passage of the Act of Pennsylvania creating a State Commission, which was signed June 22, 1891. By Section 5 of this Act, "The Board of World's Fair Managers are hereby empowered to adopt such rules and regulations as may admit the World's Columbian Commissioners and the members of the Board of Lady

Managers of the World's Columbian Commission from the State of Pennsylvania, or their respective alternates, to be ex-officio members of the Board of World's Fair Managers of the State of Pennsylvania."

It appears, therefore, that Mrs. Lucas' powers continued to be primarily those given by the Act of Congress, and in accepting the work of the State Commission she did not in any way withdraw from the larger field to which she was originally appointed.

It is, however, quite apparent that no other State made such provision as was here made for signalizing the Woman's Work of Pennsylvania. Immediately after her appointment under the Pennsylvania statutes she began the systematic work intended to be executed by the several

County Committees of Women. But she gave to the whole of it the most vigorous personal attention, removing difficulties and perfecting all the details until it came to be complete in the form now published at Harrisburg.

The title of this report is very expressive in itself of the scope and broad purposes of the work done by the State Committee of Woman's Work. It is—" A Condensed Statement of the Work done by Women, in Instruction, Reform, Philanthropy and Missions, during one Fiscal Year, in the State of Pennsylvania. To which is added a Statement of the Industrial Work of Women in the State, with Statistics. Compiled under the auspices of the State Committee on Woman's Work, for the World's Columbian Exposition, 1893: Harriet Anne

Lucas, Chairman; State Committee on Woman's Work for Pennsylvania."

This work is prefaced by a complete list of the Presidents and Secretaries of the several County Committees, the full committees in each case being given at pages 64 to 77 of the "Pennsylvania Book of the World's Fair," put forth early in 1893. The several County Representatives were there designated as "Ladies' Auxiliary Societies," in some cases numbering twenty to thirty members for the larger counties. This method of organization did elicit the most general interest and the greatest activity in almost every county.

The scope and purpose of the whole movement giving to the ladies of the country an almost equal participation with men in the great work of repre-

senting the advancement of the age at the World's Columbian Exposition, is most strikingly shown in the words of Mrs. Lucas' introduction to this volume of the results for Pennsylvania. Brief as the sentences of this introduction are, they are most impressive from their simplicity and from the elevation of thought which they embody. As the last work of the hand of this noble lady, falling almost helpless from the fatigue of a lifetime of elevating labors, they constitute an imperishable monument to her honor.

" Introduction.

" When the United States Congress called into duty the women of the country, by appointing from each State and Territory two lady Commissioners to act coöperatively and equally with men in the formation of a United States Commission,

for the creation of the World's Columbian Exposition, to commemorate the Four Hundredth Anniversary of the discovery of our country, an honor was conferred upon women such as has never before been bestowed by a government.

"It placed women at once, in this great international effort, on an equal footing with man, in the work of developing the great enterprise and bringing her tribute to lay at the world's feet, in many new forms of labor and duty, in which we find her engaged.

"It was a noble and generous action, thoroughly, however, in harmony with the broad and liberal sentiments of our Constitution, which in its one hundred and sixteen years of trial has developed the most progressive nation in the world.

"Pennsylvania was equally liberal in its action towards the Woman's National Commissioners—calling them into co-operation with the State Board for the World's Fair Exposition—and thus the State Committee on Woman's Work was formed.

This Committee at once organized County Committees for work in their own districts among the women, and thus a network of busy women covered the State, acting in behalf of their sex, and bringing to the front much that could not have been otherwise gathered.

"These statistics of the silent work done by women cannot be shown in the concrete exhibit, and while they will only prove approximate, they will serve to show how her hand and heart worked together in sustaining the weak, relieving the oppressed, instructing the intellect, to beautify the world with the development of taste and art, and ennobling the aspirations of life, until the world of nature is transformed into the world of goodness and beauty."

It is clearly a duty in the present case to make further record of the influential position accorded to Mrs. Lucas by the Managers of the World's Fair, almost

from the outset. To do this completely and to present all the evidences of desire for her aid, and respect for her coöperation, which were actually sent to her, would be difficult, because many of them are now beyond our reach. Many interesting letters are, however, where we can refer to them, and will be cited here.

Mrs. Lucas appears as a correspondent of the Lady Managers at Chicago, from the outset, ready with her suggestions and encouragement, and responding to their request for assistance. Letters from Mrs. Lucas to them, unfortunately are not preserved, but the responses of Mrs. Palmer, President, Mrs. Susan G. Cooke, Secretary, and others, appear frequently, from February, 1891. The management of the Woman's Department at Chicago was in constant correspon-

dence during the years 1891-2, and all the communications express the most ready and grateful acceptance of suggestions from Mrs. Lucas, as well as communicated to her all the leading points in the work they were then directing. I therefore give a few of Mrs. Palmer's and Mrs. Cooke's letters during that period and down to March, 1893.

It also appears by the circulars issued early in 1891, some of which are herein quoted, that the original plans and direction were practically her work, as she was the most active member of the original National Commission.

The Act of the State Legislature organizing the State Board of World's Fair Managers, was passed June 22, 1891, and was therefore second to the creation

of a Board under the Act of Congress of April 25, 1890. Under that first-named Act Mrs. Lucas had been given official position as Lady Commissioner for Pennsylvania. The Act of the Legislature confirmed that authority and made it responsible to the State.

The original authority, therefore, was that of the Act of Congress of 1890, and Mrs. Lucas' action was from the outset on the broadest field of National duty in the advancement of Women's interests in the highest sense.

The letters that happen to be available for this purpose are several from Mrs. Bertha Honore Palmer, in 1891 to 1893, and also from the National Secretary, Mrs. Susan G. Cooke, covering the same period. They are incidental rather than direct, perhaps in their

illustration of the points here made. Of course the only purpose is to recognize the unselfish earnestness of Mrs. Lucas, and not to claim any responsibility on the part of their writers.

# Correspondence Relative to the World's Fair Commission.

———

It is evident from the correspondence of the officers, both of the National Board and that for Pennsylvania, that Mrs. Lucas was the most active in suggestion and the most fertile in resources of any of those named on either Commission. Her knowledge of the actual condition of the several interests which should be represented was promptly made known to her associates, and as promptly accepted by them. It was this remarkable facility in framing plans on an extensive scale which gave her the prestige from the

outset, and made her services permanently valuable.

There is hardly an instance in history in which a leading and directive part has been taken with such efficiency and with such valuable and permanent results. This position was recognized from the outset by the successive officers of the entire Commission.

From the very organization in 1890, every attitude of the case shows such distinguished service on her part that history will give her the leading position as an actual Director of the World's Fair in all matters coming under her reach. While nominally the Woman's Department, and the distinction adopted in Pennsylvania for Woman's Work, there is no narrow limiting line, which makes it less interesting or valuable to the entire public.

Office of the Pres. Board of Lady Managers,
World's Columbian Exposition,

Chicago, February 20, 1891.

My Dear Mrs. Lucas :

I learn from one of the correspondents in the " Publicity " Department of the Exposition that, during our recent meeting, one of the ladies from Philadelphia, who was particularly well informed about the matter, gave quite a detailed description of the difficulties with which Philadelphia had to contend when preparing for the Centennial, and said our trials and delays were small in comparison. The Publicity Department is anxious to have a long and graphic article written on this subject, and so I write to ask if it was you who made the statement referred to, and if you would be willing to write the desired letter ?

I have volunteered to write and ask you, even though I know you are a very busy woman, and I myself have few moments to spare.

Of course you have heard the good news that our building has been granted us, to cost $200,000.

I shall send out in a few days an informal report to our ladies. So much time having elapsed since our meeting without anything

apparently being done. President Palmer, and the Commissioners, have advised me not to appoint the committees until the Candler report has been acted upon.

Hoping that your work is progressing favorably in your State, I am,

Most cordially yours,

Bertha M. H. Palmer.

———

Chicago, March 19, 1891.

My Dear Mrs. Lucas :

I have received your very interesting letter, and I learn with regret that it was not you who gave a reporter the interviews on Centennial work. Any report that you can have written about the inside of the work done for the Centennial will be greatly appreciated. Our path now seems relatively smooth before us, as we have been recognized and given an appropriation by Congress, and the Board of Control, which met this week, has given us ample powers and opportunities to develop any work that we may have in contemplation. I regret that you are such a very busy woman, for I fear that you will not be able to give as much time and thought to our work as we would like to claim from you.

I learn with interest what you have done in connection with silk culture, and I feel that your experience will be of great value in our work.

Hoping to hear from you soon, I am,

Yours most cordially,

Bertha M. H. Palmer.

———

Chicago, October 3, 1891.

My Dear Mrs. Lucas :

The marked copy of the " British American," is received and I have read your eloquent remarks with the greatest pleasure.

The happy way in which you presented the plans of our Board, after an able résumé of the progress of women through the centuries, could not fail to arouse the interest of all your listeners, and I feel that we are much indebted to you for this address.

Trusting that you are entirely rested from the strain and fatigue of our meeting, and thanking you once more for you valued aid, I am,

Most sincerely yours,

Bertha M. H. Palmer.

My Dear Mrs. Lucas:

Through some delay your letter was received only on yesterday.

I do not wonder that you think the delay long in sending out the minutes. I was extremely anxious to print them as soon as possible after our meeting. It was decided to issue a manual, said manual to contain everything of interest pertaining to our Board. I requested this then to be printed for information.

Mrs. Palmer was absent for two weeks and I was not willing to take the responsibility of printing. We, however, sent out various reports, pamphlets, etc., which I fear from your letter you have not received.

The standing committees were not appointed during the session. Mrs. Palmer requested the ladies to send in their preferences when they received the classification report, which I re-mail you at once. Miss Beck presented your resolutions, and I enclose type-written remarks.

I also enclose the blanks from the Director-General's office. If these do not afford the

desired information, pray let me hear from you again.

I omitted to say that Mrs. Palmer has not announced the standing committees. Many thanks for your very kind personal inquiries, which I regret to say I cannot answer in the affirmative, as I still feel very anxious regarding the minutes.

If I can serve you in any possible way, dear Mrs. Lucas, pray command me. I regret the delay in your receiving the pamphlets. There must have been some mistake, as we always check off all names.

Very hastily and sincerely,

Susan G. Cooke.

———

(Copy of Circular.)

Chicago, September 10, 1891.

Sir:

I have the honor to transmit you herewith a copy of the following Memorial, adopted by the Board of Lady Managers, at a session held Monday, September 7, 1891, and ordered forwarded to the Presidents of the various

World's Fair State Boards and to the Governors of those States that have not yet made appropriations.

Very respectfully,
Susan G. Cooke,
Secretary Board of Lady Managers.

———

At the meeting of the Ladies' Board of the World's Columbian Exposition, held in Chicago, September 7, 1891, a full report of the work done by the several States, and their attitude towards this great enterprise, was made by the National Commissioners to that body.

The animus of this most exhaustive and interesting report was one of general interest and coöperation; general but not universal, for in it we discover that several of the States have not recognized their National Lady Commissioners, and have not made any effort, by appropriations, to enable their States to take a representative position with their sister States at this great Exposition of the World's Industries; and being in hearty sympathy with our sisters from all the States and Territories, and aiming for a complete and exhaustive expression

of all the National wealth and products of our great county, and the progress of the women in their many valued lines of reform, as an expression of the voice of this body, be it therefore

Resolved, That a Memorial, setting forth the importance of Woman's Work in the interest of the Columbian Exposition and urging the appointment of women, including the Lady Managers, upon the several State Boards, be sent by this body to the Presidents of the various State Organizations, without delay, and to the Governors of those States and Territories where no appropriations have been made, giving them power and means to take their position with those more favored Commissioners whose States have thus honored them.

Mrs. Robert B. Mitchell,<br>
Mrs. John Lucas,<br>
Matilda B. Carse,<br>
Committee.

———

Chicago, October 28, 1891.

My Dear Mrs. Lucas:

Your letter of the twenty-sixth is just at hand. I regret so much to hear of your great

affliction. I was not aware of any illness in your family. I think you are very patriotic to do so much in World's Fair Work with so much illness in your household.

I trust you received my letter of recent date, explaining the detention of our minutes. The vouchers were at first detained in Secretary Dickinson's office, until most of them had been received in order to send all at one time to Washington.

I send you the enclosed type-written statements, which Mrs. Palmer desires sent to the Press in all directions. I think the first paragraph answers your inquiry in regard to exhibits. Director-General Davis said to the Executive Committee, at a recent meeting the morning after our Board adjourned, that all applications, in his opinion, should go to the State Departments when his Department received them, the State Board would be notified and will have a complete record of what has been offered and installed. If the applications are first sent to the State Board they can be accepted or rejected before coming here. However, I understand that up to the present time no such rule has been established.

The committees have not yet been appointed or rules established to govern the work of our building, (the Woman's Building) Mrs. Banks who compiles articles for the Press, in the office of Promotion and Publicity, has just informed me that nothing has been decided regarding the hospital. Mrs. Palmer left here yesterday on a trip to Texas. I will present your views on the subject as soon as she returns.

I trust you have received the reports recently mailed to you. Mrs. Banks assures me that the ladies of our Board will hereafter receive the weekly "slips" issued from their office. Trusting I have replied explicitly to some of the various inquiries that interest us all, and hoping to hear from you soon and often, I remain with great sympathy,

Very sincerely yours,<br>Susan G. Cooke.

———

Chicago, November 6, 1891.

My Dear Mrs. Lucas:

Mrs. Palmer has returned and has resumed the duties of her office. I submitted your inquiry regarding the model hospital. She suggests that you send in some proposition from Philadelphia

hospitals ; she will gladly receive suggestions, as nothing has yet been decided. The Manual has gone to the printer for the last time, I am quite sure.

I wish all our ladies realized how much I regret this delay, and that it was caused through no fault of mine that they did not receive the Minutes a month ago. My work was completed a week after our Board adjourned.

I trust your health is improving. With best wishes and sincere regards, I remain,

Very truly yours,<br>Susan G. Cooke.

———

Chicago, November 18, 1891.

Dear Mrs. Lucas :

In reply to your highly esteemed favor of the sixteenth instant, I mail you at this time, under separate cover, three copies of the Classification Pamphlet and Report of Classification Committee.

Please find enclosed an item which will probably interest you, in regard to the Indian Women in Arizona and New Mexico. We hope to keep the members of our Board fully informed in future, and you will receive the

regular Bulletins issued by the Department of Promotion and Publicity, as well as some we intend to get up ourselves.

I do not feel myself in a position to answer your questions in regard to the Women's Exchange of Philadelphia, and I suggest that you put them in regular form, and submit the whole to Mrs. Palmer, upon her return from Boston, which will be in about ten days.

We mailed the Manual to all the members of the Board yesterday. Hope you have received your copy and find it interesting reading.

Very truly yours,

Susan G. Cooke.

———

Chicago, June 7, 1892.

Dear Mrs. Lucas :

Your favor of May 31 is at hand. In regard to the Exhibit of Ecclesiastical Embroidery, I cannot say what disposition would be made of it as to place in the building, as all these subjects will be decided by the Committee on Installation yet to be appointed. The separate Guilds should make application by filling out one of our blanks. They can state their wish to be

grouped together, but it is impossible to say now whether the idea can be carried out.

We are in daily expectation of the arrival of the panels from Pennsylvania, as Mrs. Jones wrote that some were ready to send, but your letter explains that you wish to forward all together. The time will be extended to suit your convenience, as we have been obliged to do in a great many cases.

In regard to the matter of securing space we would like to assure your County Committees that their application blanks are properly cared for under the following routine: Applications for Exhibits of Women in the Main Buildings are sent to this office. I endorse and sign them, to show that they have passed through the hands of the Board of Lady Managers, and they are then referred to the Secretary of Installation, Mr. Hirst, of the Director-General's staff, who, in turn refers them to the proper Department under the classification. They reach their proper destination through our Board, and are classified and distributed as above. After having been referred to the Chiefs of Departments, notice is sent to applicants of the

disposal of their blanks, and that further correspondence will be conducted with the Chiefs of the Department to which they have been assigned.

It gave me great pleasure to call upon your friends from Pennsylvania, and I only regretted not really making their acquaintance, but hope they will be here again. Shall take pleasure in delivering your message to Mrs. Baxter.

Thanking you for your kind wishes, which have been more than fulfilled, I remain,

Very truly yours,<br>Susan G. Cooke,<br>Secretary.

———

Chicago, June 28, 1892.

My Dear Mrs. Lucas:

Several letters have come to me in the past few weeks opposing the appropriation for the Silk Industry Exhibit, and it has been intimated that our entire appropriation will be opposed in case we insist on asking for a sum for this purpose. I beg that you will write me a history of the Industry, stating also what the opposition is to this movement, and why it should be

opposed, for I am quite uninformed as to the motive that leads to this protest.

Please let me hear from you as soon as convenient, as I want to be fully informed on the subject. It would be most unfortunate to have our appropriation opposed by naming one item of expenditure which would receive so much antagonism. I have been led to understand that the representatives from Pennsylvania itself will oppose our bill, if we insist upon retaining this item.

In case Congress should give no funds for making an exhibit of the Silk Industry, have you thought of any other plan, and is your Association preparing to make a showing?

Most cordially yours,

Bertha Honore Palmer,
President Board of Lady Managers.

———

Chicago, July 20, 1892.

My Dear Mrs. Lucas:

Your long and interesting letter in regard to the Silk Industry in this country is received. I hope you will write me why you call your Association a National Organization. Is the

California Association allied to yours, and have you also branches in other States? Please let me know in regard to this point fully.

Thanking you for your prompt replies to my inquiries, I am,

Most cordially yours,

Bertha Honore Palmer.

———

Chicago, August 22, 1892.

My Dear Mrs. Lucas:

Your letter of August 16th is just received, and I write very hastily to say, that as our appropriation was reduced from the estimate we furnished, to a considerably less sum, by Congress, I fear that we shall not have any money to aid the Committee on Silk Culture. None of the committees are to receive any financial aid from our meagre purse.

I am very sorry to hear that you are not well, but trust you will be quite recovered and able to attend our meeting in October. No matter how able your substitute may be, we will feel that she cannot fill your place.

I shall write more at length later.

Very sincerely yours,

Bertha Honore Palmer.

Chicago, August 27, 1892.

My Dear Mrs. Lucas:

Your communication enclosing blanks for the Woman's Hospital Exhibit has been received, also your letter of August 23d.

Thank you very much for your kindly offers of assistance towards the collection of statistics. I trust our Board will meet in October, when you can present your most excellent plan and no doubt many will be glad to accept your method and suggestion.

As soon as Mrs. Banks, from the office of Publicity and Progress, returns from her vacation, I will request her to write an article for the papers relating to your Hospital Exhibit.

Mrs. Palmer returned from Europe about the middle of June. She has been spending the month of August, with her boys, at Camp Elsinor, Adirondacks. She writes that she spends the most of her time out of doors on the Lake; she, however, manages to keep up with our work, and has just sent for her secretary and stenographer.

In regard to our funds, Congress appropriated $110,000 for the use of our Board. I trust

you are feeling quite yourself these days. With continued regards, I am,

Yours very sincerely,

Susan G. Cooke.

---

Chicago, March 3, 1893.

Dear Mrs. Lucas :

We were very glad to hear from you again after the long silence caused by your recent illness, and trust that you are now quite recovered.

Mrs. Meredith is now in Chicago, her duties as Chairman of the Committee on Awards making it necessary for her to take up her constant residence here. She can be addressed in care of this office.

We send you, under separate cover, the tags, labels, etc., as requested, also a copy of the Minutes of the Sub-Executive Committee. We are very busy preparing the examination of the exhibits on the 15th, but will say to you that for articles of the first order of merit, about which there will be no doubt, we will give until the first of April. It is the great bulk of the more common work that is wanted for earlier examination, so that if in

any particular case more time is needed for anything really excellent, you can exceed a little to the limit. Trusting to hear from you as before,

I am very truly yours,

Susan G. Cooke.

---

Philadelphia, September 17, 1891.

Mr. Benjamin Whitman,

Executive Commissioner:

Dear Sir: I found on my desk this morning your numerous letters of September 14th, and three of September 15th, for all of which I thank you and for the information contained therein. In response I would say, first, that this letter is written on the letter-heads which were suggested and prepared by the original Committee on Woman's Work as appointed by the State Board and whose names appear above. I would respectfully suggest that we waive another letter-head until such time as this Committee on Woman's Work is perfected, and thereby made more effectual and active. I did understand that Mrs. Jones and Miss McCandless were, by vote of the State Committee, added to the Committee on

Woman's Work, and hope this also meets with your pleasure as it did with the majority at the last meeting. Seems to me that it is the only way in which we can have effectual meetings which will represent Woman's Work from the different committees. It seems to me this would have been a better arrangement than having any of the ladies on other committees, they should feel that from all the committees the proportion of Woman's Work done in the lines which they represent will be committed to the care of this Committee on Woman's Work, hence there would be a better concentration of effort and better material created for the report or catalogue, than by spreading the few women we have through the committees.

I would also suggest here that I should very much like the names of those ladies who are representative women, such as Miss Emily Sartain, President of the School of Design for Women in Philadelphia; Mrs. McHenry Cox, of the Indian School, or Mrs. Mumford, of the New Century Club (a club of women who took their existence from our Centennial) or any other representative women who have been

active in any one line of interest where good work has been accomplished; of course I do not offer these ladies in nomination, I am only writing to you suggestions which I should be very glad to have carried out. The want of action on the part of others puts me in the unenviable position of arrogating to myself more than I desire or feel capable of carrying through, besides the unpleasant position of appearing to work too personally and not collectively with other women. I hope that you fully understand my position.

Answering your first proposition in reference to ladies from our counties as Auxiliary Committees, may I ask one question? Is it probable that the Chairman of such Auxiliary Committees could be allowed traveling expenses, say quarterly, or half-yearly, to report work at the meetings of this committee, or would any such requisites be allowed? Referring again to this subject, do you think it would be probable that a resolution from the Women's Committee asking for a pro rata share of the whole appropriation, say, one-thirtieth, or one-sixtieth, to defray the whole expense of the Women's Committee, we

using our own judgment as to the privileges granted to the Chairman of the Auxiliary Committee? Of course, thus far we are perfectly satisfied with what the State Committee has done; but still as the work progresses other expenses will arise which may not be suggested to us now, and if such resolutions could be passed, the Women's Committee would take care of their own work, and the expenses accruing thereto. This desire to have representatives occasionally from these Congressional Districts was my reason for simply suggesting one lady as Chairman; she, in any way she conceives best, to form another committee of any number such as would represent the work of that district in women's line.

I observe you say one for each county, as I believe there are sixty counties and thirty-two Congressional Districts. Would it not limit the work a little more to make a District Representative, instead of the county? Please understand this only as a suggestion. I regret that I was unable to answer by return mail, as my family are still out of town. I come to the office two or three times weekly, and

found your letter on my return to-day. I would be very glad to have the names forwarded to me just as soon as possible, as we are growing eager for perfect organization and distribution of information.

For Philadelphia I would respectfully suggest Miss Emily Sartain, Directress of the School of Design for Women. I have a circular passing out to the large bodies of representative women, asking for delegates from their bodies to act with this committee, and find several answers to-day, saying that the letter will be considered at the monthly meeting in September. So that until these letters have been answered I don't wish to name any other Philadelphia ladies. I wish I had a copy of your report. Is it to be printed, and may I have it as soon as possible? Also all printed matter which the State has issued, as I feel greatly in need of having something to guide me, and having left Harrisburg hastily did not bring that which was placed upon the desk.

Referring to your second clause, I thank you very much for the interest you have taken in asking for me from the National Com--

mittee, the printed matter, and will notify you of its reception. I have already received one copy of application for space, but that was sent only to my Association and not to the World's Fair Committee. To your third clause, we wish to open correspondence with these Auxiliary Committees, and this is what we are eager for, and will forward to them our circular, to the women of the State, and any details which we may receive. In what we prepare for the State alone I would certainly feel that it should be necessary for us to confer, and will take no steps without meeting you. Should you be coming to Philadelphia, please notify me of the date, and I will endeavor to meet you at this office. Should I feel it necessary to call for you I will kindly ask for you to come, that we may prepare such form as we may require for the rapid development of the work.

I enclose to you a circular which I am about to have printed for the women of the State, but which I will defer having printed until I have your approval and authority. My intention was to send this to the newspapers to be printed and circulated to all bodies of women throughout the State, representing socie-

ties or organizations, and especially to the chairman of the District Auxiliary Associations as soon as I have their names. If you think it best that we should advise together and prepare another circular, I will defer the immediate printing of this until you write me your approval; also it would be better to defer the printing of letter-heads until we can have the names of the Chairmen of the Auxiliary Committees, and probably make the existing committee more effectual by substituting active people for those who are now inactive.

Fifth clause. If you think I could do anything by talking with the women during any part of the State Fair at Bethlehem, I would be willing to run up for a day and do so, although at present I am not quite well.

Sixth clause. I would thank you very much if any matter coming to your office on Women's Work would be immediately forwarded to this office. As you again refer to letter-heads, I think we had better defer them for the present, and can no doubt in the new ones improve the quality.

I thank you in behalf of other ladies of the committee and in behalf of the work

which I hope we shall accomplish, for your kind expressions of confidence, and for granting us full correspondence with you on any points where we may feel to need your advice,

I have the honor to be,

Yours respectfully,

Harriet Anne Lucas.

———

Philadelphia, July 8, 1892.

Dear Sir:

Having seen some of the issues of your paper, and having noticed that you have offered some space for notes on the World's Columbian Exposition, I desire to forward you a copy of a number of circulars which have been issued from time to time by the State Committee on Woman's Work (whose office is as above) for the instruction and information of our County Committees. We should esteem it a great favor if you would promulgate some of the items of information from these circulars to the women of the State through the columns of your paper. We should also be very glad to answer questions of interest that may arise in your mind which you should desire to know, in reference to the

representation of Woman's Work at the World's Columbian Exposition. We are especially anxious to arouse business women who are making their living through their own business firms to make an exhibit, as this opportunity offers to women a broader field than in former exhibitions for presenting her goods in competition with men's work.

We may from time to time send you many interesting items in the progress of our work if you can give us the space for such information.

Yours truly,

Harriet A. Lucas.

———

July 8, 1892.

Circular.

It is recommended by the State Committee on Woman's Work, to all women who are individually offering work for exhibition at Chicago, or to associations of collective exhibits, to fill out application blanks intelligently, giving a full description of the size, material and kind of work involved in the exhibits, these blanks are to be sent to the Secretary of your County Committee.

A faithful record will be kept and you will in due time be notified to what point your exhibit is to be shipped for final destination to Chicago. Do not give yourself any trouble about where or how it will be placed, as in this great Exposition this decision rests with the Classification and Installation Committees at Chicago, and we cannot change the plans and scope of these committees.

Every exhibitor must be careful to attach to the piece or pieces, their full names and address, the value of the article, if to be sold, and whether or not they shall be placed in competition; this last suggestion is imperative, as without this, it will be impossible to know how to return the goods to their rightful owners. From these statements a faithful record will be kept by the County and State Committees. To adjust all the goods at Chicago .does not rest with this committee, but with the general Commission.

If exhibits represent business interests, the State is not responsible for these exhibits, but individuals must be at the expense of preparing such protection for their exhibit as they will need, but applications for space must be

proceeded with as above directed, whether or not the individuals provide the proper cases of protection for their goods.

Trusting that these explanations will make you feel entirely comfortable with regard to the careful distribution of your personal and collective exhibits.

Yours truly,

Harriet A. Lucas.

———

1200 Walnut Street,

January 23, 1893.

My Dear Mrs. Lucas:

You are more than kind in taking the trouble to write to me. I called simply to pay my respects, and do not need to tax you by business matters. It gave me genuine pleasure to tell your daughter the kind appreciative remarks which I have heard in Chicago. I was there but two days, and during both, the thermometer was 14 degrees below zero. Our State Building is in all ways admirable, and far on towards completion. Besides that I saw only the Woman's Building and the Horticultural. Things looked

well advanced, and people talked hopefully, but there is an undercurrent of cholera scare.

I do indeed agree with you that the County Committees are a valuable body and worthy of consideration. It was delightful to again come in contact with them at Mrs. Brock's. Mrs. Brock herself spoke appreciatively of the work which you have done. I met Mr. Brownfield on Tuesday at the private view of the pictures intended for the Fair; his son and mine are old friends.

At the end of a busy day I have only time to scratch off this in acknowledgment of yours. Believe me, my dear Mrs. Lucas, that the patient endurance which you so evince towards those about you will have its reward.

Faithfully yours,
Matilda Hart Shelton.

———

Philadelphia, February 13, 1893.
Dear Mrs. Lucas :

I have your letter enclosing circular in reference to Advisory Committees, also the kindly caution in regard to overwork. I never come to the office without feeling it is of direct

use, there is really a great deal to do. I find Miss Russel, and Miss Ford, admirable helpers, and the work with them goes on smoothly.

The extra key for 1224 Arch Street will be sent to-morrow to Mrs. Eltonhead. The Silk Culture Association meet at 11 o'clock on Thursday; this I learned from Miss Russel. If you should prefer any other time than that for sending your man for some books, please name the time and Miss Ford will be there.

The receipts for Dormitory stock will be forwarded.

I greatly regret that there are so few exhibits booked from business women in Philadelphia, and not more from artists in public and private studios. Were it not that I am told that it is too late to receive more applications for space, I would indeed take active measures by applying to them direct, but the time has gone by.

When in Chicago, Mrs. Palmer spoke to me about the great advisability of having New York assume charge of the Colonial Exhibit. Mrs. Trautman also spoke to me

on the same subject, and expressed the same view. I said I agreed with them, if Mrs. Kidder would consent to the plan. They said it might be a great relief to her, owing to New York being likely to have a large amount of funds for the purpose. In New York I was recently told that they hoped to put aside $10,000 for the Colonial loan. In that case I feel they can do it better than any other State. Your letter to the Congressmen will go out to-day.

The room at 1224 Arch Street will be open to-morrow from nine to eleven, and Miss Ford will be there.

Yours truly,

Matilda Hart Shelton.

———

Harrisburg, March 10, 1893.

My Dear Mrs. Lucas:

In response to a note from Miss Ford, in regard to the printing of the statistics, would say, that the whole work can be printed here, and of course it should be done here, since there will be no money to spare from the Women's Fund. You speak of wanting the book bound like the special copy, in morocco. Suppose you

would only like a few copies so bound; the rest would have paper covers, like our Pennsylvania book. I should think 10,000 copies would be amply sufficient to go around, but you might be the best judge of this.

You will simply have to express the manuscripts, plates, etc.; we would take charge of it, and have it printed for you.

At the Executive Committee meeting, last night, I brought up the subject, and your number of letters bearing upon the Silk Exhibit. All favorable; offered nothing against it, and spoke strongly in favor myself of the exhibit. I told them you claimed that this exhibit was planned while you were acting head of the Women's Work; that you had made your arrangements and obtained space; that it was too late to talk of giving it up; that I personally believed it would be a very interesting exhibit. Mr. Buchanan was of the same opinion, etc. They however, on account of scarcity of funds resolved to lay it over until our meeting next week, and, in the meantime, request me to obtain from you further information. Governor Watres' resolution in brief was: "That the Executive

Commissioner be requested to ascertain how far we are committed to this Silk Exhibit; whether Mrs. Lucas has made arrangements and promises which commit, etc." I told them that I thought you had; but you can write me a letter which I may receive before the time named.

We were very sorry not to see Mr. Blodget; he did not put in an appearance. Possibly he may come to the next meeting, seven o'clock Thursday evening, which is called to discuss finances and further appropriation. No action was taken about your position in the Board, for the reason that that has never been disturbed. Your title is just the same as it always was; it was simply resolved that the work was to be turned over to Mrs. Shelton, and all responsibility pertaining thereto; and as I have already told you, if the Executive Committee were your brothers, it was just what they ought to have done. All feel kindly toward you, and at any rate you know well that I do. I cannot say more than that, for I am very sincerely

Your friend,

A. B. Farquhar, Ex.Commissioner.

Harrisburg, March 16, 1893.

My Dear Mrs. Lucas:

It was proposed that we give $1,000 to the Children's Home, sometime since, though it was never definitely turned over. This $1,000 I am going to divert to you for the Silk Exhibit. Presume it would meet your approbation. It would be of more interest to Pennsylvania.

Our work seems to be going on very nicely now. You will be glad to hear, and if Mrs. Shelton does not work herself to death we will probably make a very creditable exhibit.

Mrs. Palmer writes that she is going to give us all the time possible, but the exhibits all ought to be there early in April, and they should know immediately the amount of space wanted.

We have a meeting of the Commission to-night. Am sorry you will not be able to attend.

Yours truly,

A. B. Farquhar,

Ex. Commissioner.

Harrisburg, March 23, 1893.

Dear Mrs. Lucas:

It is always pleasant to know that we have friends. Yesterday I told you to go ahead with

the Silk Exhibit, if the funds could not be furnished otherwise, you might command them from me individually, and upon my return home, I found the enclosed telegram from Mrs. Palmer, which relieves me entirely.

They have plenty of money now I believe in Chicago for the Children's Home, and everything else.

I send you the dispatch, for its kind words of you. Hoping that you are better, I am,

Yours truly,

A. B. Farquhar,

Ex. Commissioner.

---

Wilmington, N. C., February 7, 1893.

My Dear Mrs. Lucas:

Your last letter, with a copy of the one you purpose sending your Representatives, is at hand, and I hasten to notify you of the fact that the petition has at last gone to Senator Ransom, who I trust will take prompt and immediate action in the matter, so I shall be glad to have you send your circular letter as early as possible to your Senators and Congressmen, and I am sure such a letter coming from you will carry its influence. And let me

thank you, my dear Mrs. Lucas, for your compliment to me, which I feel all undeserving, but which I greatly appreciate. I received a few days ago a letter from Mrs. Troutman, saying that the New York State Board was going to make a proposition to me, which she advised my accepting, and this morning's mail brought me a letter from the Secretary of the Local Committee presenting the proposition as follows:

"You are authorized to say to your committee that it is proposed that New York take charge of the Colonial Exhibit of the whole country, and assume the care and protection thereof, provided, the State of New York make the appropriation in the bill now pending in the Legislature, and provided that the Board of Lady Managers of the World's Columbian Exposition appropriate $25,000 for that purpose and place the amount at the disposal of the Colonial Committee of the Woman's Board of Lady Managers from New York, and provided the exhibit can be made in the Government Building."

Now what do you think of this proposition? It is a question that of course I cannot individually decide. I shall put the proposition before the seven States who have signified their inten-

tion of uniting in a co-operative exhibit and each must decide for itself. I fancy the States which have no funds to meet the expense of a Colonial Exhibit will be glad to get under the wings of New York, but I doubt very much if a great State like your own will accede to this plan. So I write first to hear the voice of Pennsylvania upon this important project.

Very sincerely yours,<br>Florence H. Kidder.

———

Wilmington, N. C., March 7, 1893.

My Dear Mrs. Lucas:

Knowing your feeble health, it is always with reluctance that I impose one of my letters upon you, but not only as a member of the Centennial Committee, but also because you are so helpful and suggestive to me, do I often feel the impulse to write to you.

I received some days ago your communication enclosing Mr. O'Neil's. I refrained from answering it at once, because I have been waiting further developments, and also awaiting some authentic information from Senator Ransom about our bill. I have not heard direct from him, but heard from my

friend and alternate, Mrs. Cotten, who is representing me on the Federal Legislative Committee, now in Washington. She writes me that we will not get our $25,000 appropriation. I fancy from what she writes that it was simply referred to the Committee on Appropriations, and never did go before either the House or the Senate. I do not state this authoritatively, but it is only an inference; however, the fact remains that the Fifty-second Congress has adjourned and we did not get our money.

There is but one thing left for us to do, and that is to unite the Colonial Exhibits of Pennsylvania, New York and North Carolina, with the addition of heirlooms from Territories and States other than Colonial. And I have had the offer of many historic relics from California to Maine. From Montana comes the offer of a most interesting collection, and the State Board will pay all costs. Our North Carolina State Board has given not a penny to the Colonial work, but through my individual effort and personal appeal to our people, I have collected a sufficient sum for all expenses for insurance, transportation, etc., and we can

make a most interesting and historic display. I am seriously thinking of going on to New York and Philadelphia next week and see if I cannot make arrangements with the Colonial Committee of those States, and have them consent to a united exhibit of the three States. Do you think it advisable that I should do so? Please tell me frankly.

We have so little time to lose that what is to be done must be done promptly, and letters are at the best unsatisfactory. I have had some correspondence with Mrs. Frederick R. Jones, of the New York Board, and she thinks that both Massachusetts and New Jersey could be secured for a united exhibit, although their Representatives on the Colonial Committees, Mrs. French and Miss Russel, answered that their articles would go with their building.

I shall be glad to have a line from you as to the practicability of my seeing the New York and Pennsylvania State Boards.

I beg that you will pardon this hurriedly written letter, which, I fear, you have scarcely found legible.

Very truly yours,

Florence H. Kidder.

My Dear Mrs. Lucas:

I am sure Mrs. Gillespie, who was in Washington with Mrs. Troutman and Mrs. Cotten, has told you of the space accorded us in the rotunda of the Government Building, and that it is decided to place our Colonial relics there. The necessarily limited space greatly curtails the plan and scope of our exhibit, and I cannot carry out my original plan of a large and comprehensive display in the Woman's Building. But I fancy it will be more unique and historic, and more in keeping with the dignity of the Government, and with the assurance of Government protection.

I find the apathy which has heretofore pervaded many of the States has been dispelled, and many whose exhibits were to be placed in their State buildings will now make a Colonial display in the Government Building.

The space allotted us comprises six alcoves, thirteen feet wide and three feet deep with about fifteen feet of wall space. The idea was to apportion one alcove to two States, but I think there will be many of the States which

will make no Colonial display, and this, of course, will give the others an extension of room. I do not believe that either Georgia or South Carolina will come in. In my own State, North Carolina, I have by individual effort raised the amount necessary to cover the cost of our Colonial display, which I trust will be interesting.

I hope you have had sent you from Washington the blue print, showing our position in the Government Building. It is in close proximity to the Department of State and of Justice, where will be displayed the Declaration of Independence, the Constitution of the United States, and many other kindred documents.

The whole building will be patrolled night and day. The Board has reserved the right to pass in detail upon all the articles exhibited, and the display will be subject to all the rules and regulations of the Government Board, both as to the selection of the articles and the manner of installation.

Very truly yours,

Florence H. Kidder.

Rome, Italy, March 29, 1893.

Mrs. John Lucas, Philadelphia:

Dear Madam: I beg to submit to your approval the following report concerning the work done in Japan to interest the ladies of that country in the Woman's Department.

Upon my arrival in Tokio I had a long talk on the subject with Mr. Edwin Dun, Charge d'Affaires ad interim of the United States, who told me that up to that time (March 1892) it had been impossible to interest the Japanese in the Woman's Department. He was very anxious to do all he could, but he did not think that the Government and the Imperial Commissioner were in favor of a Woman's Exhibit. Yet, he thought that if the Empress could be interested in the matter she might do something, as she is very liberal and progressive; but he considered it impossible to approach her, and was convinced that no woman in Japan would take an interest in the Exposition unless she should first approve of it. Mr. Dun told me that the address by you to the Empress had been sent to him by the State Department, and that he had given it to H. E. Yashitane Sannomiya,

Vice Grand Master of the Ceremonies of the Imperial Court, whom he considered the best man likely to be interested, as he had traveled much, is very progressive and liberal, and that his wife is English. I requested Mr. Dun to introduce me to Mr. Sannomiya, which he kindly agreed to do. The following morning he took me to the Imperial Household, where I had a long talk with Mr. Sannomiya. Your letter had not yet been given to Her Majesty, but he promised me that it would be presented to her at once. I told him what the Government and ladies of the different European countries were doing, which interested him greatly.

Two days after, being Madame Sannomiya's "at home," I called on her, accompanied by a mutual friend, General Legendre, Vice Minister of the Home Department of the King of Corea. Madame Sannomiya did not think that the women of Japan would possibly have anything to do with the Exposition, and to use her own expression, when she spoke of it later, "she simply sat on me," and told me I was losing my time. She and the other ladies, whom I met afterwards, were convinced

that the Japanese women had nothing of interest to send.

Two following days I studied the matter deeply, found many things of interest, which could be sent by the Japanese ladies—not only their beautiful work, but that of the women of the poorer classes, and many things to illustrate the schools, hospitals, Society of the Red Cross, etc.

I found out that women had had much to do with the History, Literature and Arts of the country, and armed with many suggestions, and a better knowledge of the question, I called again on Madame Sannomiya; in fact, I called several times, and from that time she became a warm supporter of my plans—though she had little hope in their success. One day she exclaimed: "If the Empress could only be interested." It was clear that nothing could ever be done unless the Empress should approve. But to approach her was declared to be an impossibility by the United States Minister and all my friends.

I had taken with me to Japan a powerful stereopticon apparatus and views of all the places of interest in the United States, and

also views of all the buildings, palaces and gardens of the Exposition as they now appear. I proposed to give a lecture before their Majesties—a proposition which made most of my friends smile as it was considered altogether impossible.

Napoleon said long ago that "impossible" was not French, and very fortunately it was French I had to use in my dealings with the Court. Meeting every day in a social way persons connected with the Court, I did not lose an opportunity of getting nearer and nearer, and after several weeks of difficult, delicate, strategetical and diplomatic manœuvres, I succeeded in being received by their majesties and delivered my lecture before them and the ladies of the Court. This success I owe greatly to the efforts of Mr. Dun, Mr. and Madame Sannomiya and Marquis Kido. The lecture was such a success that the United States Charge d'Affaires sent a special telegram about it to the State Department. In the lecture I said all I could in favor of the Woman's Department, showing views and plans of the buildings and a photograph of the President. Her Majesty was very much interested, and a few days afterwards I had the

pleasure of hearing that she was thinking of appointing a Commission. I had been charmingly entertained at the Palace, and the Emperor was so pleased with the views that he sent me for presents two fine pieces of Cloisonnè, by Namikarva, the great Japanese Artist. At that time I left for China, and was absent nearly one month. Upon my return I received a call from Marquis Kido, Master of Ceremonies of the Court, who brought the good news that her Majesty had appointed a Commission composed of the most prominent women of Japan. Furthermore she had given from her own purse the money to carry on the expenses of the Lady Commissioners. I said at the beginning of this letter that the Imperial Commissioners were against the appointment of such a Commission. They were especially afraid to have to pay the expenses of the Government's appropriations. But when they saw that the Empress herself was interested, and would furnish the money, they changed their minds and became warm supporters of the Ladies' Commission. Mr. Sannomiya, and Marquis Kido, were appointed by her Majesty as advisors to the Ladies' Commission. Marquis

Kido, frankly admitted that it was a new work to him and to the ladies. I suggested that I might be able to advise them and to explain what was the aim and purposes of the Woman's Department. My proposition was accepted at once. Princess Mari, called a meeting of the ladies at one of the Imperial Palaces, and there I had the honor to address them. After giving them a full history of the Woman's Department, I explained what had been done in other countries, and suggested many things which could be done successfully by Japanese ladies. I showed them plans of the buildings, explained that the Exposition would be divided into several rooms, and that therefore it was necessary for them to decide at once upon the amount of space they needed in each room. After they had offered me a delightful supper, the ladies decided that they would need one thousand square feet. I knew it would be difficult to give so much space, and as it was absolutely necessary that the ladies should know as soon as possible whether they could have it or not before beginning their work, I promised them that I would see you personally and cable them how much space you could afford to give them.

Upon my arrival in Chicago I heard that you were in the Adirondack Mountains, and the Secretary, Mrs. Cooke, told me that she did not think that the Japanese women could be given more than four hundred feet. I immediately decided to see you in person, and went to Paul Smith's, in the Adirondack Mountains, where I had the honor to report to you.

After our interviews I was able to cable to Mr. Sannomiya, "eight hundred feet assured, probably two hundred more later." Two weeks later I sailed again for Japan, where I found the ladies delighted with the space given to them. Her Majesty and the most prominent ladies of Japan, were taking great interest in the Exposition. I called the attention of these ladies to the presence in Tokio of Mrs. Frederick Winston, and suggested that she might give them some advice. A reception was organized by Mrs. Coombs, at the United States Legation, where Mrs. Winston met all the lady Commissioners. A few days afterward (the evening before my departure) Princess Mari entertained at dinner Mrs. and Mr. Winston and myself; at that dinner all the members of the Commission were present.

This is, Madam, how the Lady Commission of Japan was formed. Thanks to the interest of her Majesty, to the efforts, first of Mr. and Madam Sannomiya, and Marquis Kido, and then to those of Princess Mari and other ladies, it will doubtless send a most interesting exhibit.

I am most happy to have been able to do this much to thank you for all your kindness, and for the interest shown me by the Board of Lady Managers.

Believe me, Madam,

Yours very respectfully,

A. B. de Guerville,

Honorary Commissioner.

At the request of Mr. de Guerville, who is ill, the above report has been copied and forwarded to you.　　　　　　　B.

———

428 South Thirteenth Street,

Philadelphia, April 10, 1893.

My Dear Friend Mrs. Lucas:

I am very very sorry to hear that you have been so ill. I hope you will be better soon, and will be able to teach our Chinese friends again.

If it is not so, of course our Heavenly Father knows what is best for you and us all. I visited your Sunday-school yesterday afternoon. I must say you have faithful teachers at your school, I met many of them whom I had met before, and I am often thinking of my warm friend Mrs. Lucas, who has done so much for our countrymen in this Christian land. Shall we not appreciate your kindness ; certainly we will not forget your kindness, what you have done for our men before. I am sure we are greatly indebted to you for your kind heart, lady. May the dear Lord bless thee, and keep thee.

With kind regards to you and family.

Very faithfully yours,

Moy Shoo Po.

___

May 1, 1893.

My Dear Mrs. Lucas:

The Auxiliary of Bucks County have just held a meeting to take a résumé of our work, and to act upon the proposed "Permanent Organization;" but I feel that I cannot draw the work to a conclusion without a note of thanks to you for your very acceptable and cordial help through the difficult parts of it. I received

your last circular, and fully understood and appreciated your position, and felt sincere regret that your health had prevented you from continuing in active work to the end, and finishing what you had so successfully planned and carried on almost to completion.

I thank you personally for your prompt and helpful response in all times of difficulty, and assure you that your kindness will be one of the pleasant memories of the occasion.

The committee join with me in expressions of appreciation and thanks.

Believe me, very sincerely yours,

(Miss) Louise H. Smith,
Chairman Berks County Aux.

———

Chicago, May 4, 1893.

Dear Nellie:

From Miss Ford I hear of the extreme illness of your dear sweet mother. She has been so lovely to me, and, Nellie dear, my love for her is strong and I know she was fond of me. It does seem hard that neither General McClelland or your lovely mother could see the consummation of their hopes.

I wrote a long letter to your mother, but feared that reading might worry her. Mrs. Shelton has carried out our plans, and Pennsylvania is behind no State. Instead of ours, I should have said Mrs. Lucas' plans.

Give your mother much love, from her attached friend,

Mary E. McCandless.

———

143 East Thirty-fourth Street,<br>New York City, May 5, 1893.

My Dear Mrs. Lucas:

In a letter which I received from Miss Mary F. Smith, a contribution from you toward St. John's College was enclosed with one from her. I want to say a hearty "thank you" to you, and tell you how much I appreciate your remembrance of my work. It is very kind of you in the midst of ill health to think of me and of St. John's College.

I wish I could have met you and talked over the work among the Chinese in America, for I am told you inaugurated the Chinese Sunday-school at Epiphany Church.

You will be glad to learn that so far I have secured over $14,000 of the $20,000 I want to

raise. I still hope to be able to raise the balance.

Hoping this will find you in better health, and that it may please God to spare you for many years to come, to carry on the work for his Kingdom, I am,

Yours sincerely,

(Rev.) F. L. Hawks Pott.

————

Philadelphia, July 20, 1893.

My Dear Mr. Lucas:

I sincerely appreciate your sending me the Memorial Sermon. I read it with much interest last evening. It is a beautiful tribute to Mrs. Lucas' memory, and the record of her life as given by Dr. Stone, should be an incentive to all her friends.

Yours sincerely,

Wm. M. Coates.

————

Erie, Penna., July 29, 1893.

Dear Sir:

If you can conveniently, be kind enough to send me a copy of the Memorial of Mrs. Lucas,

a notice of which I see in the Philadelphia papers. I am one of those who greatly honored Mrs. Lucas, and remain true to her memory. Excuse haste and form, as I am just leaving home, and write at the depot, in order that I may not be too late to receive a copy.

Yours truly,

Benjamin Whitman.

———

No. 112 W. Fourteenth Street,
New York, June 14, 1888.

Mr. Lorin Blodget:

Dear Sir: Your letter, with others, I received just as I was coming away for a short visit to my son in New York, and I take this spare moment to thank you for your kind appreciation of my effort in behalf of " Home Missions." I greatly believe there is a missionary spirit in me, which while God has given me a Home Mission to do in my family, also finds (for I do not really seek it) a duty to many not of that household, but of the great brotherhood of God. The Chinese, a race which it seems to me, God has placed in the direct line of duty for this American people,

the Italians, who are now forming a composite part in daily and public labor in our large cities, (see Carl Spreckel's work) and in any other work or race who may cross my path, and need my advice, or any helping hand.

Is not this the Mission Christ came to teach? I can find no other, not of creeds and doctrines, etc., though all those as He and His Apostles—so Divinely taught—I respect and revere, and these only.

I am glad to tell you that our appropriation of $5,000 for 1888–89 is secure. I fear we are not, in the Woman's Silk Culture Association, living up to our opportunities. I want to see John Cutter while he is here, I want to be a missionary to him. Do you think we could open a small plant of machinery and manufacture our own silk into underwear or knitted goods? There is a little trouble in regard to our market for the silk we have. Call on Mrs. Souder and ask her to see a copy of my letter just sent to Cutter. Remember Strange, Tilt, Dexter, Lambert and others.

I would like to talk to you on my return next week. My sons at Garden City, Yale

and Sing Sing, are having commencement exercises this week for which I am here.

Yours truly,<br>Mrs. John Lucas.

# Summary of the Results of Woman's Work.

The Report of the Woman's Work Committee for the State of Pennsylvania, forms a volume of 135 pages, in which the results of the examination made by that committee are stated with full details first, and ultimately in the summary form.

This report is of itself a marked departure from the usual exhibits of charitable and industrial occupations. The intention is to give the distinctive work of women, and it will surprise all ordinary readers to find so many institutions for Instruction, Reform, Philanthropy and Missions. Full descriptions are given of one hundred and forty-six institutions of this class, founded and directed by women; the name, the location, the date of founding, the name of the Principal, a brief

of the purpose of each, and the means of support being given in each case. In the first portion of the volume a description of the building and a handsome engraved design is given for most of these institutions. The leading facts in the history and the founding of these institutions, with the names of those connected in any manner with the direction are given in each case. This report, therefore, constitutes a complete directory to all institutions chartered for the purposes before named, in the State of Pennsylvania, founded by women.

The educational features of several of these institutions are also prominent, and they are all designed to elevate and instruct all their beneficiaries, so as to fit them for active life as independent citizens.

This department of the work done by women closes with page 100 of the report, with the tabulation showing the total work done by one hundred and forty-six institutions.

The second portion of the work relates first to "Industrial Statistics of Women's Work in Pennsylvania." In this portion a summary is given, first of the textile industries proper,

and next of book publishing and printing and the lighter industries, there being in Philadelphia 1001 establishments of this class, employing 74,946 women and 75,744 men, with 15,645 classified as youths. There are, therefore, fully 83,000 females to the 83,000 males, or an equal number of each sex. This is really a very remarkable change from the condition of things ten or fifteen years since. It is undoubtedly true that in the regularly compensated employments described as industrial, or engaged in creative labor rather than in merely routine or servile labors, that there is now an equal number of women and girls receiving fairly liberal payment, at least in all other than the great iron works. And in most cases the surroundings are made pleasant and attractive and the working girls are as careful in dress and manners as could be desired. While not paid quite as much for their labor as men and boys are paid, the difference is not large and is only on the part of men who have positions of direction or of management.

This report also shows what great improvements in the employment and compensation of women have been introduced with the silk

and silk-mixed goods manufactured. Most of these mills are comparatively new, and there are over seventy in Philadelphia alone and over thirty in the smaller cities and towns in the Eastern part of the State. This report being for 1891, there are about ten thousand women and girls reported in the eighty-five silk mills then existing. It is remarkable that the American methods of weaving silk are wholly conducted by young women, while the Lyons silk fabrics are woven by men alone.

A detailed list of the silk mills and those on fine mixed goods in Philadelphia is given on pages 106 to 118, this list being made from the return of the factory inspectors for that year, and generously furnished to the Woman's Committee by the Lady Inspectors. Further lists of silk mills and of most other fabrics employing women in the Northeastern and Northwestern and Northern counties, are also given on pages 109 to 112. These new and most interesting details being also furnished by the Lady Inspectors for the year 1891. A recent law placed the inspection of these factories, in which women are employed, in the hands of lady inspectors, and they have

discharged their duties of inspection with remarkable firmness and success.

The Woman's Committee, therefore, performed a most valuable service in bringing out the facts as to the industrial employment of women and girls. Their report shows the most striking change in this respect, and that even in Pittsburgh and Allegheny City, and in the iron and steel works and glass works particularly, a large number of women and girls are employed.

In Pittsburgh and Allegheny alone the numbers reported are 3842 women and 1717 girls, in a total of 53,242 of both sexes employed in one hundred and eighty-six mills.

In Lancaster and York Counties it is surprising to find that the number of women and girls employed in the greater industries is much in excess of the number of men and boys.

The next division of this report includes a summary of mission work in the churches, which gives some new and valuable statements of the leading work of each denomination in each of the several counties of the State.

Some interesting details conclude the report, in the designation of the literary women of the State, and the principal works of which they became authors.

## Review of the Official Minutes of the Committee on Woman's Work.

The extent and completeness of the plan laid down by Mrs. Lucas for representing Woman's interests at the World's Fair was very remarkable. A report of the proceedings of the Congressional District Delegates, representing the State County Committees, held at Philadelphia, November 30, 1892, affords the most ample and instructive proof of the value of Mrs. Lucas' direction and the effectiveness of her plan of work.

For the general purpose of the Woman's Exhibition, at Chicago, the State appropriated $10,000, with a further appropriation for specific purposes of $5,500. This general appropriation was practically controlled by Mrs. Lucas, who was Chairman of the Committee on Woman's Work. The plan was so large and generous

as to bring into active co-operation a committee in each county. This extension of the working machinery, as it may be called, necessarily involved contributions of articles and even of expenses on the part of such County Committees. The cost of gathering the results and of transmitting and putting in form at Chicago, was the principal use to which the appropriation would be placed, and so careful and economical had the management been, that up to December 1, 1892, only $1,800 had been spent by the Woman's State Committee. There had, however, been a diversion of $2,500 to the Art Committee, $2,000 to Miss Garrett's School, $1,000 to the Children's House, leaving $8,200 on December 1, 1892. These facts are stated only to show that this singularly effective and complete organization of county committees cost very little indeed. It was most wisely directed at the outset and most honorably conducted throughout.

The extended report of this final meeting of thirty-two pages must be consulted to show the real magnitude of the work.

Every page of this report shows the original and directive force exercised by Mrs. Lucas.

She presided at the opening, and, indeed, she directed at every stage of the proceedings the succession of events. She called on each responsible officer in turn, first those of the State Commission, and next those of the County or District organizations, bringing out in each case the amount and character of the preparation and of the exhibits to be made. This report itself is very instructive, because it shows most remarkable developments of artistic, professional and practical skill on the part of prominent women in the State in almost every county. Any one who had no precedent in such cases would see here the fullest vindication, both of the purpose to make such exhibits, and of the capacity of the women of the State to do honor to the occasion, and to show that an enlarged department of actual science, of artistic and professional skill, as well as of mere skill in the industries and in education, actually exists on the part of the women of the State of Pennsylvania. It was therefore a duty to elicit these facts and to make them a part of the State's exhibit, and it is not too much to say that both in design and in execution this

work is to be credited to Mrs. Lucas above all others.

The following extracts from the official minutes of the meeting of the Congressional District Delegates, held at Philadelphia, on November 30, 1892, give the leading points of the direction exercised by Mrs. Lucas:

Mrs. Harriet A. Lucas, of the State Committee, presided. After a brief opening address by Hon. John W. Woodside, Mrs. Lucas then introduced the Executive Commissioner, Hon. A. B. Farquhar, who made a short address. Then followed the introduction of Miss Mary E. McCandless and Mrs. Yarrow. After the roll-call of delegates from each of the twenty-eight districts, Mrs. Lucas informed the ladies that reports would be read in the order of their Districts. As this extremely interesting succession of reports proceeded, Mrs. Lucas explained the especial features in many cases.

Mrs. Lucas stated that Chester County would exhibit the Convent work of that County, and it was explained that Philadelphia would not encroach on Chester County's exhibit of Convent work. On a request by Mrs. Wade, of Pittsburg, as to the order of the several reports,

Mrs. Lucas informed Mrs. Wade that as the business of the meeting was to hear State reports, the whole State would be heard from in the order of their Districts.

The Chester County Auxiliary Board reported some very important collections; also the Delaware County Board, which had sent a carved panel to decorate the Women's Building at Chicago, and a block of Delaware County Granite, cut in the shape of a keystone.

Mrs. Lucas spoke of the letter which the Pope had sent to Mrs. Potter Palmer, offering to distribute copies of it, and hoping it would induce the Convents to exhibit.

A report from Mrs. Wilson, for Bucks and Montgomery Counties, embodied some very important statements, showing the establishment of many institutions in those counties, controlled or founded by them. Other eastern counties were, in some cases, extremely well represented, while the mining counties of the East and North were not so fortunate. Northampton County, however, was rich in antiques and Colonial relics.

Mrs. Lucas suggested that Monroe County send photographs of its scenery.

From the Ninth District, important reports of silk mills and other industries were given. In most cases the personal efforts of the ladies of the committee, secured the desired information. From Lancaster County, the artistic representation was the statue of Maud Muller, and other pieces of equal merit. Also from this county report was made of a woman's owning and publishing a newspaper.

Careful and complete reports were made from Schuylkill, Lebanon, Dauphin and Perry Counties. It was reported that 80,000 women were represented in the Fourteenth Congressional District, many of them being employed in the finer and more valuable industries.

The Lebanon Industrial Works employ 1200 women, and the silk factory at Harrisburg employs 350 women. Dauphin County reports many leading charities, and Lebanon County reports an art school and a school of art needlework, both of which will send exhibits. Large numbers of women profitably employed were reported from all these counties.

Various reports from the interior counties, Bradford, Susquehanna, Wayne and others, were next made; in some cases without obtaining

much to exhibit. In Potter County however, some valuable artistic work was reported and fine needle-work, also embroideries. From Clinton County a silk quilt of original design, made of the badges of the Women's Relief Corps in the United States.

Mrs. Lucas suggested that from agricultural counties, the committees should endeavor to have the agricultural work of women exhibited.

Columbia County's exhibit in the Woman's Building was prepared chiefly of silk fabrics, done wholly by women employed in the Bloomsburg Silk Mill. Sixty women employed in that mill received the same wages as men so engaged, the work being managing silk looms.

A volume of poems was reported, composed by Miss Drinker, of Bloomsburg; also designs for decorative work in laces, carpets, etc., by Miss Wooley. Miss Wooley will design a carpet to be woven by a woman in the Bloomsburg Carpet Mill. The Normal School of Blooms-burg will be represented by twelve girls in the joinery or carving of native woods. The Woman's Auxiliary of Huntingdon, report a fine stained glass window, made by a young

lady. For Franklin and Juniata Counties, fine artistic work will be produced.

For Cumberland and Adams Counties Mrs. R. H. Thomas, made an important report, specifying the several exhibitions at Atlanta, New Orleans, and elsewhere, and declaring their purpose to co-operate in making the World's Fair of 1893 the crowning glory for all World's Fairs.

From Carlisle, Cumberland County, valuable reports of Memorial Buildings erected by women, were made.

From Cambria, Blair and Somerset Counties, interesting reports of the employment of women, were made, but exhibits were not important. A report of active efforts in Westmoreland, Armstrong and other western counties was made. Some suggestion being made that the entire collective exhibits could hardly find room, Mrs. Lucas assured the committee that it would be received, but perhaps not collectively placed.

The report from Allegheny County was especially full of striking illustrations of the advancement of Women's Work. The exhibits will be artistic, literary and educatioual, from a large number of the bright women of Pittsburgh and Allegheny.

From Washington County an advanced state of educational and artistic progress was made.

Very interesting exhibits were reported from the remaining counties, much exceeding the anticipations of the original committee, but apparently fully sustaining Mrs. Lucas' original plan.

Mrs. Lucas, at the close of the reports of the Congressional Delegates, commended the women of the counties for the varied and admirable reports they had made, realizing that the scattered nature of the work of women in the counties had made their duties in many respects arduous and complicated, and expressed her satisfaction at the variety and interest of the statistics and the exhibits offered.

She felt that the plan of interesting the ladies of the counties had been excellent, inasmuch as it had brought many of the women of the State together in one common interest; she expressed her hope that there might be a grand re-union of Pennsylvania women at the coming Exposition, and that we shall all meet together in our State Building as the promoters of woman's interests on high and broad grounds for her further advancement and success in life.

The session closed with the transaction of many items of executive business and with some important directions made by Mrs. Lucas. She directed that badges be secured for members of committees, and a sub-committee was appointed to receive any such designs. She also directed that two books be collected from each authoress, one for the Library in the Woman's Building, the other in the State Building, with a sketch of the life of the authoress. Further directions were given by her that the bills of expenses should be sent to Philadelphia, where they would be paid. She also proposed to originate a Colonial Memorial Museum, to preserve the historic relics that might be exhibited. An account was then reported by her Secretary showing a balance of $8,199 still remaining of the entire appropriation of $15,500, the larger share of which had been given to special committees as before stated. This was almost the complete duty of direction required at the hands of the committee originally, and the subsequent work was confined to the faithful execution of the plans so perfected by the direction of Mrs. Lucas.

## Papers in Review of Mrs. Lucas' Work.

The personal manuscripts of Mrs. Lucas are remarkable for the evidence they afford of her persistent efforts to secure a continuance of the aid of the Government to the development of the silk industry in the United States.

These efforts were especially directed to the obtainment of some form of appropriation in the Session of 1890–91. She addressed leading members of both the House and Senate, as well as the chairman of the leading committees, with the most conclusive arguments, writing to Senators Paddock and Allison. She had also written in September, 1890, to Secretary Blaine, as well as to Mr. McKinley, who had succeeded Judge Kelley as Chairman of the Ways and Means Committee. The principal reason for the failure of these efforts was the open and determined opposition of the silk manufacturers of

New Jersey, who preferred to rely entirely upon imported raw silk, and who did not content themselves with passively awaiting the growth of silk in .the United States ; they opposed such growth to the best of their ability at all times.

Mrs. Lucas had no interest whatever in any partial development, or in the progress of the silk weaving alone without benefit to the farmers and producing interests of the United States, and her broad-minded purpose was thwarted by the narrowness and greed of these Paterson silk manufacturers in the first instance.

Another and perhaps equal reason for the failure of Congress to appropriate in these later years, 1890 to 1892, was the inordinate demands of Managers of the Silk Culture office at Washington, of the Bureau, as it hoped to be, for the Promotion of Silk Culture formed in the Department of Agriculture.

A complication of offices with excessive salaries was to be established there at an annual cost of $150,000, and bills appropriating this sum, with an elaborate detail of services, were reported at each Session from 1888 to

1892. They could not be, and ought not to have been, agreed to by Congress, and as the Department would accept no less, the whole system fell, and the work has been abandoned by that Department. A moderate and proper course of action on the part of that Department would undoubtedly have secured the approval of Congress.

# The Silk Exhibit at the World's Fair.

It was the especial desire of Mrs. Lucas, both for herself as a Directress of the World's Fair, and for the Women's Silk Culture Association, to secure a working exhibit illustrating the production of silk from cocoons and the weaving of silk fabrics.

There was much difficulty in obtaining any specific appropriation for this purpose, and still more difficulty in obtaining the proper space for the loom and ·reels. All these difficulties were overcome, however, the small space offered them in the Women's Building was applied to another purpose and a much larger space was given them in the Agricultural Building, about 18 x 30 feet, in a very favorable position. This space has been very handsomely decorated, rich flags, woven by this Association, and a very effective silk reel is constantly at work,

with their Jacquard loom, weaving ribbon souvenirs, which are readily sold to the visitors.

The interest in the reeling, especially, is very great, and crowds are at all times in attendance; it has, therefore, been very satisfactory to the Managers of the Building and instructive to the public.

The appropriation obtained by them was $1,000 from the State appropriation of $300,000, and this sum would have paid the attendants about to the middle of August; but so liberal has been the purchase of souvenirs that the profit on these will suffice to carry the whole exhibit through to the end of the Fair. Miss Ford is entitled to great credit for her skillful management of the questions as to the rooms themselves, and her intelligent management of the whole exhibit after its final location in the Agricultural Building.

There was much discussion at the several meetings at the State Board of World's Fair Managers as to the introduction of the Exhibit prepared by the Women's Silk Culture Association into the State Building. The Exhibits of Women's Work were so numerous and occupied

so much space that there were various questions raised and objections made to giving the necessary space for the machinery of the Silk Exhibit. Commissioner Farquhar took pains to obtain the opinions of the ladies of the Commission, and to adjust the matter in accordance with their wishes.

Ultimately a better opportunity, and in one sense a more appropriate one, was offered in the Agricultural Building, thus making it, in a great degree, National.

Several of the correspondents of Mrs. Lucas spoke with so much energy in behalf of this Exhibit that it would have been a grateful recognition to quote their letters here; but it may be sufficient to say that the warm interest felt in it was all justified, both by its successful location in the National Agricultural Building and by its attractiveness and value there.

# Review by Mrs. Lucas of the Work of the Silk Association, as Embodied in a Memorial to Congress, 1891.

---

To the Honorable Members of the House of Representatives at Washington :

The history of the introduction of Silk Culture into the United States, by the Woman's Silk Culture Association, whose office is at No. 1224 Arch Street, Philadelphia, is not unfamiliar to this Body, since in January, 1885, a Committee from this Association presented to your House a National flag, prepared from the pure American product; and following that presentation made application to your Hon. Body for an appropriation to the Agricultural Department for the propagation and protection of this industry; thus enabling this Association to become participants with

the Agricultural Department, and more readily pursue the object in view.

The bill in which this presentation was made was successful in securing your aid; and in the following year an appropriation was made to the Woman's Silk Culture Association of $5,000 per annum, since which, during four years, we have been able to greatly enlarge the scope of our work (acting at the same time in perfect harmony and accord with the Department of Agriculture) and embodying in our work the distributing of mulberry trees for the purpose of the industry to every part of the United States.

As the growth of trees, giving to the culturist, the necessary product for the food of the silk-worm is the primary and most important division of this new industry, we recommend this to your consideration as a special branch of our work.

We come before the Representatives of our Government in an appeal for a continuance of that confidence in our effort, which your former appropriations to us indicated, and of which we have in the last year been deprived, by the action of your Body in

giving the whole sum to the Agricultural Department.

It is the desire of this Association to continue its efforts until the close of the Columbian Exposition, with a hope that that great National event may give us an extended opportunity to form a more thoroughly National Association than has yet existed.

We have sent out 40,000 mulberry trees to every part of the United States.

We have made exhibits at forty-seven different Exhibitions, both State, National, and Foreign.

We have had upwards of 50,000 correspondents; have received at our office and instructed thousands of visitors.

Have purchased 12,000 pounds of cocoons, which we have reeled into marketable silk, returning in money to the women and children of the country, for the product of their labor.

We have presented American flags to our own State Legislature, to the National Congress, to Mexico and every Republic of South and Central America, to the cities of Atlanta, Albany, Boston and Philadelphia, and to the

English Technical School at Manchester, England.

We have sent out thousands of Instruction Books in the Art of Silk Culture to every part of the country.

We have turned the American cocoon into every silk fabric manufactured in the United States to test its quality; from this material over two thousand yards of silk fabrics have thus found a channel for the raw material.

To carry on this work we have had one paid Superintendent at $570 a year, the rent of two rooms, one as an office, the other as a reel room or filature, at a rental of $750 a year, with incidentals for printing and publishing.

You will thus see we are the faithful and economic allies of the Government, and we demand from you, as chivalric Statesmen, that you will continue to us our former appropriation of $5,000 a year, and that you grant us this appropriation, with a recommendation for its continuance.

[From the Congressional Record, January 24, 1885.]

# Native American Silk Flags Presented to Both Houses of Congress.

———

## Senate.

Washington, D. C., January 23.—In the Senate to-day the Chair laid before the chamber a memorial of the Women's Silk Culture Association of the United States. The memorial recites the great success through their efforts of the work of Silk Culture in the homes of this country, and craves the good-will, influence and aid of Congress in the development of an industry so important to the women and children of the United States. The memorialists beg the Senate to accept, with their memorial, a truly American national flag, made of silk raised in American homes, by American women and children, reeled, spun,

dyed, woven and mounted in Philadelphia. The flag, which is a large and handsome one, was borne to the desk, and was the subject of much admiration, both from the floor and the galleries.

Mr. Beck offered a resolution expressing the high appreciation and thanks of the Senate for the flag, and admiration for the efforts and success of the Women's Silk Culture Association in their patriotic purpose to ameliorate the industrial condition of their countrywomen, and to enlarge and diversify female employment in the United States.

Mr. Morgan, in a feeling and happy manner, welcomed the flag, with all that it meant, to the hall of the Senate.

Mr. Dawes congratulated the country on the great advance made in silk culture in so short a time, it being only a few years since the work was undertaken.

Mr. Beck's resolution was then agreed to.

### House of Representatives.

When the House met to-day a handsome silk American flag ornamented the wall behind the Speaker's chair, and after the reading

of the Journal, the Speaker laid before the House a communication from the Philadelphia Women's Silk Culture Association of the United States, tendering the flag to the House of Representatives, and bespeaking for it a place in the Hall of the National Government.

Mr. Kelley (Pa.), offered a resolution, which was adopted, accepting the flag prepared for the use of the House, and presented by the Women's Silk Culture Association of the United States, and declaring that the excellence of the fabric and perfection of colors it displays afford evidence of the remarkably rapid development of the culture and manufacture of silk by the American people, and that the House will cause the flag to be displayed within the halls of the House.

## Presentation of Silk Flags to the Pan-Americans, Washington, April 11, 1890.

———

A goodly company, comprising the entire number of the delegates from South and Central America and Mexico, and the Hon. Secretaries, Rusk, Tracy and Windom, met a committee from the Women's Silk Culture Association of the United States, and a large number of Washington ladies and gentlemen, to witness the presentation of seventeen American flags, one to each free State represented in the Pan-American Congress.

Professor Boswell, of Dickinson College, presided, and after a few well-chosen remarks, introduced Mr. Beaseley, who made a fitting and patriotic address.

Mrs. John Lucas, President of the Women's Silk Culture Association, then made the presentation address, alluding to agriculturists, and suggesting silk culture as a prominent and practical one for the agriculturists all over the

Middle, Southern and Western States. She referred to the lamentable ignorance of the people on the subject generally, and suggested a small duty on raw material, which could only increase the value of silk goods a few cents per yard. This would form a splendid revenue with which to establish in our country educational and experimental stations, where silk culture could be scientifically illustrated, as it is in European nations.

She stated that no former efforts had been made, when surrounding conditions were as at the present time, a nation rich, progressive, advancing in taste and art, in elegance and wealth, and demanding the best and finest of goods. There should be silk manufacturing communities, having not less than four hundred mills, with sixty millions of capital, and perhaps 250,000 workingmen and women, all turning out the golden threads of silk for the use and adornment of the race. $25,000,000 now annually leave this country for raw silk as raw material. No past condition offered such a picture.

In closing she said: "Gentlemen of the Sunny South, bear with you these emblems of

the success of our Nation. Place them in your Legislative Halls, and ever regard them as tokens of one hundred years of national prosperity of a government 'of the people, for the people, and by the people,' and the devotion of a little band of women to the advancement of home production and industrial education."

Response of General Bolet Peraza, Delegate of Venezuela.

Ladies :

I thank you in my own name and that of my colleagues for the gift we have just received at your hands.

This is the emblem of your country, the glorious ensign of this great American nation, with whom our respective Republics have just sealed a family compact.

Upon reaching these shores, seven months since, that flag greeted us as strangers ; to-day it bids us farewell as brothers.

It reminds us also of the origin of our independence, because it was those stars and stripes that dazzled the imagination of our indomitable grandsires, and which imbued their patriotism with the desire to gain for their sons the same liberties the fathers of your

sovereignty acquired for you. And to make this emblem still more valuable and significant in our hands you have endowed it with the prestige of your labor, which can be compared only to that of the indefatigable insect who, by his labor clothes in splendor all the world.

You, generous Ladies, have founded a new and rich industry for your country. The day will come when the United States will compete in the production of silks with China, with Persia, with France and with Italy, and they will owe it, in great part to you, who have given hospitable shelter to the modest worm, who have nurtured it with assiduous care, and who, by your devotion have induced it to give you its silver threads, its golden skeins, which you have woven for your brothers of Latin-America into these flags, emblematic of the heroism of the men and the noble worth of the women of this great people.

To our homes will we carry this precious gift of yours, and there will we place it by the side of our country's flag, united and connected as are already the interests and the destinies of all the free countries that brighten the continent of Columbus.

# Address of Mrs. Lucas at the Convention of the Saint George's Union.

Oswego, N. Y., April, 1891.

The fifth toast, "Women of the Nineteenth Century," was most eloquently responded to by Mrs. John Lucas, of Philadelphia, Pa. Her address occupied twenty minutes, and the audience listened with deepest attention. It was replete with biblical and historical reference.

Mrs. Lucas said she would be recreant to the faith she had in the purity and permanence of the progress of women during the nineteenth century, and the elements that have led to it, should she hesitate to defend her position and admit her real emancipation from the thralls that had environed her during many ages of the world's history. To trace and unravel the mysterious manner in which

she was given to man, shows conclusively
that the Divine will was "as part of man,
bone of his bone," that man should be
satisfied with her; that he should accord to
her the same honor and care that he would
lavish on his own body; co-equal with him
in honor and power—but looking to him as
he to her, and bound to him—links in the
great chain of common humanity. Man, the
projector of a greater and higher form of
creation; woman, the mother of all.

The speaker touched at length on the early
history of woman as we receive it in the
Mosaic history, as proof of the honor and
dignity to which she was called, while yet
God dealt directly and personally with His
chosen people. From history, Mrs. Lucas
quoted Helen of Troy, Andromache, Lucille,
and even Cleopatra, as examples of woman's
love and devotion not to be forgotten.
Coming down to the Christian era she referred
to the martyrs among women. Down among
the ages we find a gradual emancipation of
women going on until the Renaissance. After
this period, and with the rise of English
learning and literature, we find stately Elizabeth

on the English throne, grappling with such problems as shook the religions of the world, and opened unto us a reformation from the circles that had seared and tarnished the purity of the Apostolic Church.

To her wonderful force and intellectual ability we owe this blood-bought and priceless gift—a pure gift. Through the line of literature and art, as it developed in this golden age, woman, as author and artist, destined to live forever. The speaker alluded to the life of women in the home, in the factories, in social and the lower walks of humble home-life, in all of which she casts her strength and influence, and moulds the race.

Mrs. Lucas alluded to a phalanx of notable women—Lady Blessington, Rosa Bonheur, Mary Wortley Montague, George Eliot, Mrs. Browning, Katharine Tait, Charlotte Brontë, Siddons, Rachel, Jenny Lind, Patti, Scalchi as examples of women in the fields of literature and the stage. As explorers she mentioned Lady Baker and the indomitable Mrs. Peary.

Speaking of women in the branches of industry, Mrs. Lucas said that in Massachusetts statistics show that women have secured a

footing in 4,467 branches of industry. The last census in Massachusetts reported 932,884 women and 1,009,257 men employed in gainful occupations. Women working for lower wages than men may have affected these numbers, and it is well for great manufacturers to see this. Let not women become the disturbing factors in upsetting the old condition that man is the bread-winner, and through avarice and false economic views use the low-wage woman to supplant the man, leaving him to periods of idleness and thus to mischief. The rule should be "equal wages for equal work." Not doing this, tends to destroy home-life, and what weakens the home undermines the national prosperity.

The speaker paid a fitting tribute to England's noble Queen and the advancement that religion, learning, art, science, authorship, domestic and political economy have made during her reign. Mrs. Lucas referred to the available influence and ramifications of the World's Fair, as bringing forward the united results of brain and muscle of both sexes and their stimulating development. She spoke of the appointment of a Woman's Board—two

representatives from every State and Territory in the Union, on the Fair's Commission, and concluded her address as follows: "You, Gentlemen, as manufacturers and masters, do her justice; do not withhold a faithful record of her labor, when appealed to; give her of the 'fruit of her hand' and let her have 'honest praise within the gates'—for as long as the stars shine and the rivers run she will be the companion and the comforter of man.'"

At the conclusion of Mrs. Lucas' address she was warmly applauded.

# St. John-in-the-Wilderness.

## From a Manuscript in the Handwriting of Mrs. Harriet Anne Lucas.

In the year 1850 a property was bought at the village of Gibbsboro', in Camden County, New Jersey, and a manufactory of chemicals and paints started by Mr. John Lucas. In 1856 the family of John Lucas removed to this place, and there being no place of public worship, at once connected themselves with the Protestant Episcopal Church of Haddonfield, under the ministration of Rev. Mr. Hallowell, and started a Union Sunday-school at the little school-house in the village. During the years that followed, various denominations, especially the Methodists and Baptists, held service on the Sabbath afternoons at the school-house, which fluctuated in interest and attendance, but never grew into a body, which seemed animated with

a desire to establish anything permanent, and from year to year no effort was ever put forth to make the services, occasionally held, either instructive or lasting in their effects by the establishment of a place of public worship.

At one time Mr. John Lucas introduced into this Union Sabbath School an Episcopal form of service, but after a season, finding it distasteful to many (even to the fact that one old itinerant minister always remained outside the school-house until after the creed was repeated, because "he did not believe in worshiping the Virgin Mary,") and not wishing to place any of our views before the people, if not acceptable to them, this Episcopal form was abandoned, and with it Mr. Lucas resigned from the superintendence of the Sabbath School. Left to their own desires, but with the regular attendance of the family, the school passed through many variations, but was never abandoned.

Thus, after a quarter of a century of sacrificing, in a measure, our own principles to the wills of others, and suffering the privations of the precious ritual and teachings of our beloved church, we as a family felt animated to set up

our altar in the midst of these people, who thus far had never made any movement towards such an end for themselves, and in 1881 a lot was selected and efforts made to obtain it; but legal difficulties arising, a whole year passed before it was decided where the church should be built. Finally a " parcel " of land was given by Mr. John Lucas, and a subscription started by him of $1,000. Other subscriptions to the amount of $1,366.36 were collected. Plans were submitted by Mr. J. Durang, and Mr. W. D. Hewitt, Architects ; on August 1, 1882, the contract was given to Wm. Bernhouse, on the plans submitted by Mr. W. D. Hewitt.

In looking back over twenty odd years of union effort in this little village, I am led to feel we have neglected a sacred duty and made shipwreck of many blessings, which might have fallen upon this people and our own family, in evading our duty and failing to rely upon the promises of God; of hesitating to plant the Church of God, and allowing the vacillating opinions and desires of men to set barriers in the way of truth, and that fixedness of purpose and principle which are the outgrowth of truth

If our Church is the exponent of truth and the one Apostolic Church, dictated by Christ himself, why hesitate to plant it everywhere? The seed once planted in faith, can never die, and thus through sacrifices and real trials have we learned our duty, which properly sought for, would have been made plain long years before.

On Sabbath afternoon, October 1, 1882, the corner-stone of the Church of St. John's in the Wilderness was laid by the Right Rev. Bishop John Scarborough, assisted by other clergymen; the Bishop and the clergy with the Sabbath School, met at the residence of Mr. John Lucas, and thence walked to the church grounds, singing "The Church's One Foundation is Jesus Christ the Lord." Very interesting services followed in the presence of a large number of people, and an offertory of about $2,488.14 was made. In the box placed in the corner-stone was deposited, one copy of the Book of Common Prayer, one copy of the Holy Bible, one copy of the Hymnal of the Protestant Episcopal Church, one copy of the services of the laying of the corner-stone, one copy each of "The Churchman," "The Guardian," and "The

Episcopal Register," one copy of "The West Jersey Press," some small coins, and the following statement :

After a residence of many years among the people of the village of Gibbsboro', in the State of New Jersey, during which time the number of inhabitants has materially increased, and yet no church edifice rears its walls in our midst, and having in remembrance the great debt we owe to Almighty God for his continued goodness to us as a people, inasmuch as He has blessed us with peace and prosperity, and continued our lives in health ; has kept us from great evils ; it seems fitting to rear to his honor and glory, a temple for the worship of Almighty God, according to the rites and usages of the Protestant Episcopal Church in America. To this end, and with a firm reliance on the help and blessing of Almighty God, through his Son, Jesus Christ, the effort has been made and many have given of their means to the Church fund.

Faithfully relying on the sure promises of God, that he will give His holy presence to this temple and consecrate every effort here made to draw the hearts of men and women unto him, we name this Church ST. JOHN'S-IN-THE-WILDERNESS, that like as he in the weary waste and among sinful men, proclaimed, "The Lamb of God that taketh away the sins of the world," the coming of whom was to bring grace and truth ; so may the mission of this holy church be a voice in the wilderness, crying, "Make straight the way of the Lord," and become to the

careless and sinning a "Light shining in darkness," calling them to better life, and to higher and holier purposes, a very promise of good things to come.

Signed, October 1, 1882.

| John Lucas, | Harriet Anne Lucas, |
| Mary C. Lucas, | John Thomas Lucas, |
| William Edward Lucas, | Mary W. Lucas, his wife, |
| H. Anne Lucas, | James F. Lucas, |
| Harry S. Lucas, | Albert Lucas, |
| Ellen Bown Lucas, | Joseph Wilson Lucas, |
| Barton Lucas, | Robert Suddards Lucas, |
| Francis Ethel Lucas, | Elizabeth Sanders Lucas. |
| Miss A. Elizabeth Wright, | |

Architect, William D. Hewitt.

Builder, William Bernshouse.

Services performed by

Right Rev. Bishop Scarborough, of New Jersey.
Rev. Gustavus Murray, of Haddonfield.
Rev. R. Moses, Rev. Mr. Reilly.

List of contributors :

| | |
|---|---|
| Mr. William H. Lucas, | $100 00 |
| Mr. William Waterall, | 100 00 |
| Mr. George W. Childs, | 100 00 |
| Mr. James Moore, | 200 00 |
| Mr. J. Thomas Lucas, | 100 00 |
| Mr. Alfred Lucas, | 100 00 |
| Proceeds of Fair at Lakeside | 300 00 |
| Proceeds of Tableaux, | 68 00 |
| Mrs. John Orne, | 25 00 |
| Mrs. W. E. Lucas, | 25 00 |
| Miss Carrie Lucas, | 25 00 |
| Mr. J. T. Clark, | 25 00 |
| Mr. Robert Smith, | 15 00 |
| Mr. Lewis Risture, | 10 00 |
| Mr. Ed. Rudderow, | 5 00 |

| | |
|---|---:|
| Mr. Robt. Hamilton, | $ 5 00 |
| Mr. Chas. Potter, | 5 00 |
| Mr. Albert Sayers, | 5 00 |
| Mr. C. Chalten, | 5 00 |
| Mary Hartner, | 6 00 |
| Mrs. Fred Elliott, | 25 00 |
| Mrs. James F. Lucas, | 25 00 |
| Mrs. Ed. T. Lucas, | 25 00 |
| Mrs. Wm. Rank, | 20 00 |
| Mr. Jos. Moore, | 10 00 |
| Sunday-school, | 18 75 |
| Kate Hartner, | 5 00 |
| Annie Haines, | 5 00 |
| Mrs. C. D. Thum, | 5 00 |
| Mrs. C. Stoddart, | 5 00 |
| Wm. Burk, | 1 00 |
| Mite Box, | 3 81 |
| Alexander Hamilton, hauling, valued, | 15 00 |
| Albert Lucas, | 10 00 |
| John Stack, | 10 00 |
| Harry S. Lucas, | 10 00 |
| H. Annie Lucas, | 10 00 |
| Jno. W. Snowden, | 10 00 |
| At laying of the Corner Stone, | 45 58 |

Including $1,000 from John Lucas the offerings were $2,488.14, as shown above.

---

## HARRIET ANNE LUCAS.

---

This most appropriate and earnest tribute to Mrs. Lucas' high character and noble works, has been circulated largely among her friends, and has elicited expressions among her friends which are here transcribed and to some extent condensed as an appropriate part of this more permanent form of Memorial to her honor.

# A Sermon

in remembrance of

## HARRIET ANNE LUCAS

preached in

The Church of St. John's-in-the-Wilderness

Gibbsboro', N. J.

On St. John Baptist's Day, 1893

by the

Rev. JAMES S. STONE, D.D.

Rector of Grace Church, Philadelphia

# "Her Grace is Above Gold."

Ecclesiastes vii: 19.

———

Such is the worth, says the Son of Sirach, of the Wise and Good Woman; and so impressed was that ancient man with the blessing of such a woman to her husband that again and again, in the course of his book, he pens lines which illustrate and expand the thought of our text. There seems to be experience as well as philosophy in words such as these: "The grace of a wife delighteth her husband," and "A silent and loving woman is a gift of the Lord." The writer, as though he had before him a precious memory, tenderly alludes to "the beauty of a good wife in the ordering of her house," to "the beauty of the face in ripe age," and to "the fair feet with a constant heart;" and he declares of the man that hath a virtuous wife, "the number of his days shall be double—he shall fulfil the years of his life in peace." Of the graceful woman he says,

"If there be kindness, meekness and comfort in her tongue, then is not her husband like other men." She is to him "a pillar of rest," more than friend and companion, above even children and the building of a city, and like Wisdom herself, adorned with the golden ornament and the purple lace, she shall be for him a robe of honor and a crown of joy.

King Lemuel, taught by his mother, had a like appreciation of the blameless, pure and noble woman, and he, too, after the manner of the Son of Sirach, seems to have had before him, rather than an ideal, a personal recollection, when he says of such, "The heart of her husband doth safely trust in her; she will do him good and not evil all the days of her life; her candle goeth not out by night; she reacheth forth her hands to the needy; in her tongue is the law of kindness; she looketh well to the ways of her household." Unnecessary is it to add, "Her children arise up, and call her blessed; her husband also, and he praiseth her."

"Sisters part from sisters—brothers
From brothers—children from their parents—but
Such woman from the husband of her choice,
Never."

And nowhere, indeed, does woman appear to greater advantage than in the home. God has His sanctuaries on earth—places consecrated for His worship and as witnesses to His glory; but there is no spot on earth more holy or more to be reverenced than is the home in which love and duty, sacrifice and religion, abide. And such virtues can only exist where the housewife is herself true at heart and gentle in mind and manner. The earliest refuge of man was lost by sin, and upon him fell labor and sorrow, but the All-Merciful left him his best earthly belonging to brighten the dark, sad life. Woman is never nobler or more helpful than in times of adversity; and when the gates of Eden were closed against her and her loved one, she took heart and gathered up the strength and sweetness of her God-given graces and made in the desert a new home, and trained even the weeds and thistles of the malediction into flowers of beauty and delight. Thus she created and adorned the resting-place for the weary and the heart-sore, and became for the man more than ever the helpmeet which her Lord intended her to be. Nor is there in this world anything

more beautiful, more entrancing and uplifting, than the testimony afforded to grace and virtue by two brave, pure hearts, strong in each other's love—though possibly poor both in friends and in worldly goods—struggling together along the path of duty, through the day of gladness and through the night of sorrow, towards that grand and ultimate goal of all life, heaven and God.

It is well sometimes to think of woman as, for instance, Dante thought of his divine Beatrice, and as the theologians, poets and painters of the Church have thought of her who was blessed above all daughters of earth, the Mother of our Lord. The world has never had a sweeter conception than the former, or a purer and lovelier reality than the latter. In Mary, verily. have been set forth the fullness of beauty and the sublimity of virtue ; she was pure, humble-hearted, trustful—the perfect maiden and the exalted saint; so much so that when we look at her as a Murillo or a Raphael looked at her, without going to extremes that some, swept by the forcefulness of the ideal, have gone to, we realize her to be full of grace, and memories of plaintive, softest music once heard within

the holy walls come again to our soul. But the Blessed Virgin, in the plenitude of her splendor, enthroned in the glory which an Angelico imagined was worthy of her, is far beyond the good women of whom the Son of Sirach and King Lemuel wrote, and whom we know in our every-day life. She lives in a realm that few, if any, can approach, possessing a privilege which can never again be possessed by woman; and the very glory of her character, while it encourages and strengthens every woman who looks steadily upon it, is so rich, so far away, so hallowed, that every woman knows she can never be as is the Handmaid of the Lord. Therefore we come down to lower ideals, if you will, and think of woman, not in extravagant and extraordinary phases, but in the plainer and more practical way that the philosophers I have quoted thought of her; for both you and I know that the woman and the wife as these writers of old depicted her still lives, not in rare and isolated instances, but in homes and in families beyond numbering. None of us need go far and not behold such—even more dear and beautiful than poetry or aphorism can make her; patient, true, pure, loving—her grace

above gold. And an example of such I shall show you before I have done, in the good woman whose memory we recall to-day in solemn service and in sincere affection.

What her life was is known to all, for you saw it as it was lived through the many years. Few, indeed, if any, are there present who did not know Harriet Anne Lucas—one as the loving and faithful wife ; others as the patient, sympathizing and affectionate mother ; all as the friend whose heart was ever open to the cry of the helpless, and whose hand was ever ready to give proof of the kindly and noble instincts of her soul. But warm as this appreciation may be, it is not every one who can realize the fullness of her life and character. The depths of our nature, whence flow the springs beside the waters of which grow the flowers of kindly deeds, are beyond our ordinary vision ; and I confess I think of such with a consciousness of mystery and a feeling of awe. In truth, such a study, next to the study of God Himself, is most profound. And the difficulty of it appears greater when we remember the isolation of individuality. Life itself is mysterious ; but the person is still more so. Not one of us can

tell to another all that lies within our own heart and mind. Perhaps we are not aware of the reality ourselves. But what we are, we may judge others to be—the same strange, complex creatures, doing at times the most solemn and the most beautiful things, and at other times the most careless and frivolous things; having great hopes and small hopes, curiously mingled, so that to-day we think first, say, of Heaven, and to-morrow of some trifle we are ashamed to own up to; full of ambitions, thoughts that lie deep and silent as the pools of the river, and thoughts that flit as the sunlight runs along the hillside; amiability and obstinacy, trust and doubt, firmness and irresolution, right and wrong, tangled together in strangest fashion; at one moment lifted up to heights of purity, holiness, honor and love, till angels' joy seems ours, and at the next possessed with evil so hateful that we dread lest any one should think such possible for us—a curious medley, I repeat; songs and sorrows side by side; virtues and vices growing together like the wheat and tares—such is the human heart. And down in those depths is a consciousness of the loneliness; each soul

for the most part living by itself; unable to tell to others the thoughts that are too deep for words or tears; looking upon others without power to make itself understood; pride battling with justice; and under all this the hope, the yearning, longing hope, that God will have pity and forgive, and save His child from grief and woe. Our poor, disturbed individuality, therefore, is not wholly bad, nor is it wholly good; and the outcome corresponds thereto. Man may have gone very far from original righteousness, but he has not reached total depravity; he may have grown better and truer, but he has not attained to the purity of God. As the Divine grace affects him, so does the chaos tend to order, the darkness lightens; yet so long as he is in this world in his life there will be day and night—a character exalted, but not perfect. Therefore, when we would consider a given person, we must needs remember these evident truths; and when we see the growth of a useful and a beautiful life, we must know that in the individuality— which we may not look into—righteousness is overcoming wrong, virtue is freeing itself from the cerements and bandages of evil, strength

has come to the better qualities, and God's grace is preparing the way for final triumph. This is the only trustworthy test: he who does good, and loves to do good, is good—that is to say, of course, good, not absolutely, but comparatively. And when through a long life you find the good predominates, the love holds firm, the kindliness, honor, integrity and unselfishness prevail, you may be satisfied of the strong and noble character, and of the binding of self to the Divine will.

This I have said in order that I may lead you not only to acknowledge the good works which Mrs. Lucas did, but also to appreciate and sympathize with her spirit and her life. When I apply to her the words of my text, I desire the application to be fully understood, so that in what she was, as well as in what she did, you may recognize that her grace was above gold. She had her ambitions and her visions—nor would she have been real had she been without such; but none can say that they were ambitions or visions for herself. Her longings and her hopes, her abundant labors and her persistent energy were indeed constitutional, the expression of her really

remarkable individuality, but they were put forth for the sake of her family or her friends, for the good of the afflicted and the needy, or for the glory of Almighty God. A busy, comprehensive mind was hers, running out in many directions and concerning itself with many enterprises. She was never idle : truly was it in work that she found her joy, and in toil her rest. A daughter of a mother who had no ordinary share of the poetical temperament, she inherited a love for the beautiful in nature, in humanity, in art and in books—the gift of response to the rhythmic flowings and the soulful voices of genius, so that under its influence she became impassioned, enthusiastic, excited. Her power of expression was considerable. To a degree far from common she had the pen of a ready writer, the ability to give an argument or a description clearly and simply, the readiness to discern truth, and the voice and manner to command the attention of those to whom she spoke. She was earnest and sincere, meaning every word she uttered, and holding fast to her convictions. Nor was she without skill in management, as is shown by her presence on the boards of many societies.

Other graces, too, she had, as will presently appear.

One of the objects of her affectionate solicitude was this church in which we are now gathered. Truly could she say, "Lord, I have loved the habitation of thy house; and the place where thine honor dwelleth." From the day when the foundations were laid until the hour when for her all earthly things faded away, her interest in the welfare of this sanctuary never flagged. She loved the very walls thereof; the services and the duties therein wearied her no more than shall the services and the duties in yonder land of glory. "Our little church in the wilderness," she used to say with winsome fondness; and then she was wont to add in slightly graver tone, "We must not forget our little church in the wilderness." It was very dear to her, and none the less dear will it be to you who love her. I do not know whether she ever read Wordsworth's Ecclesiastical Sonnets, or Isaac Williams's Cathedral Poems, but the spirit which touched those singers touched her also. Born and bred a daughter of the Church, she appreciated the life of the Church—that gentle life which befits the

Bride of the Beautiful Christ, but which, like the sweet grace of the wild flowers or the tender loveliness of the hidden soul, is too often over-looked, not only by the world, but also by many who have eyes to see and ears to hear. That life, divine and pure, brought to her benediction and peace, breathing into her soul a holy calm, and speaking to her of that rest into which, by the goodness of God, she has now entered. The Church, to such as comes the inspiration which came to a St. John and a St. Augustine, is personified and transfigured—a beautiful mother, robed in spotless purity; a second Eve given to the second Adam; with a voice of wondrous sweetness, and eyes that tell of heart-depths where love abides, and hands that fall beseechingly on the shoulders of the erring and soothe gently the humble and the trustful. To her come Christ's little ones, His dear children, and she loves them because they are His; and as they behold not only her clothing of wrought gold, but also her heavenly graces, they win an attachment, a loyalty which time cannot weaken and which death cannot destroy. She is from above, the Witness of God in this darksome world, and she tells us—sweet Mother

as she is—now of duty, and now of the time when her Lord shall wipe away the tears from off all faces. Such a conception can never be theirs whose Christianity is bound up in a sect and whose theology is that of a denomination. And because our beloved friend had something of this ideal, she struggled against the narrowness and bigotry which surge around us. She was a Churchwoman from beginning to end—catholic; and her religion, because catholic, was therefore historical, and because historical, therefore scriptural. So she loved, as one of her sensibilities naturally would love, the performance of Divine service and the administration of rites and sacraments with those ceremonies, many of which are of primitive origin, all of which have been consecrated by time, and in which not a few of earth's choicest spirits have found a happy expression for their devotion. So she loved, too, as one of her sensibilities naturally would love, to hear of the story, the constitution and the doctrine of that Divine society which has come down through the ages and in which dwells the Spirit of the living God. Thus she learned the truth of sacraments and the worth of

unity—of unity, not simply with Christians in the present day, but through the centuries with the Church of Apostolic days, and beyond the centuries with the Church which is in heaven. And thus it came to pass that her heart clung to this House of God, and for nothing did she wish and work more than that the people of Gibbsboro' should be gathered into the fold and be taught the ways of the Church of Jesus Christ. "Sanctified in the wilderness," as her words used to run; the wilderness which she helped to make rejoice and blossom as the rose, and never so much as when she wrought for the lifting up of these walls and the setting of the Cross upon a building that should be God's own Zion— the gates of which He should love more than all the dwellings of Jacob. Time passes away; the Cross remains, and in the coming years when we are all gone—

> "the Sun with his first smile
> Shall greet that symbol crowning the low Pile:
> And the fresh air of incense-breathing morn
> Shall wooingly embrace it; and green moss
> Creep round its arms through centuries unborn."

A woman thus devoted to the Church could not but give herself also to works which tended

to the bettering of others. I cannot tell of all
her benevolent efforts. She gave freely of her
time and means, and when her sympathies were
aroused—which commonly happened—she was
as generous of the latter as of the former. Never
turned she her face away from any poor man.
She was active in the Newsboys' Home, in the
Italian Mission, in the House of Rest for the
Aged, in the Chinese pagans of Philadelphia,
and in Indian Missions. Her public spirit
was shown in the interest she gave to the Silk
Culture Association, and in the labor she did
for the Exposition in Chicago. In fact, it is
not unlikely that the unceasing toil and the
consuming devotion she bestowed upon this
last-named enterprise shortened her days. She
organized and guided the part which the women
of Pennsylvania purposed taking in that work;
and she laid down the management and ceased
to dictate letters to her secretaries, not till the
hand of death was upon her. Gold is good,
but the grace, the self-sacrifice and work of a
wise and good woman is above gold. Verily,
when the Master rang the bell for His handmaid, around her lay the work. Long as
was her sickness, and weak as her body became,

her energy and devotion kept her at the appointed task; and when she went to Him who had called her, she went wearied and worn, labor-stained, ready, indeed, to fall asleep.

There was another love, too, she had, which was to her very sacred. Why she loved England I need not say; but with an ardency born of true affection she delighted in reminiscences of travel in that country—the dales of Derbyshire, the fields of Kenilworth and Stratford, the busy streets of London. And because she loved the quiet, shady lane, the meadow where purls the brook under the willows, the village church, whose spire points ever heavenward, and whose bells send their sweet melody far across the country-side; the manor-houses, the inns, the cottages—homes of a nation's life; and because she loved the story of that life—its romance, its grandeur, its struggles, its victories—because of all this, and much more, she cared for the work done in this country to help and relieve distressed wanderers from over the sea. With Societies having such for their purpose, she was in heartiest sympathy. She sometimes went to their festive gatherings, listened with interest to the speeches made on such occasions, and not

unfrequently herself uttered words which, because they were fervid and helpful, always were received with attention and drew forth applause.

But much as she may have cherished the memories of England, it may be doubted if a spot on earth was more dear to her than this village of Gibbsboro'. Its associations were most precious to her of all the associations of life. Here she lived, as she told me again and again, her happiest years and cultivated her choicest friendships. This was home as no other place ever really became; and as nowhere else, here she found health and rest. She did much towards reducing the dreary wild this place was when first she saw it to its present finish and beauty. In her husband's plans, whereby ultimately art triumphed over nature, she took the profoundest interest, and where perseverance and labor made a garden, love and fidelity changed it into a paradise. She was the good housewife, and within the old home yonder were husband and children, affectionate and loyal, great-hearted as herself, and friends rejoiced in the hospitality there given, and innocent merriment prevailed, and never went away man or woman thence a stranger, or with feelings other than of respect

for the lady whose grace of disposition mani-
fested itself in generous deeds. I do not wish
to imply that her life was without its difficulties
—every life has such. She had the same
complex nature which we all have, and her will
and her prejudices were strong—as from her
forceful character they could not be otherwise;
but she met her difficulties heroically, and she
proved herself worthy of being reckoned among
the wise and good women whose grace is above
gold. Nor would I lead you to suppose that
gifted though she was with impulsiveness and
imagination, she was to any appreciable degree
either contemplative or sentimental. She was
too active, too practical, too restless, and found
her days too full, to indulge in visions, sweet
though they may be. But so quick were her
perceptions, so lively her sense of the beautiful
and so exact her appreciation of nature, that
she caught instantly the thought and the charm.
say, of a poem, a painting or a landscape.
Hence she understood and loved, strongly and
really, the picturesque surroundings of her home,
How she delighted in the eventide to look
upon the serene and shimmering waters of the
lake, and to watch the bending lily-leaves, and

the splash of the wavelets, and the woods beyond, rich in their summer splendor or their autumnal red and gold, and the clouds tinged with sun-glory resting in the blue and silent sky! She loved it all—the green lawn and the spreading elm. The depth and fulness of her love were shown in the last words she spoke in this world—"'Take me to Gibbsboro.'"

It was a simple utterance, but one full of meaning. The river of memories rushing swiftly along, then overflowed its banks. "Take me to Gibbsboro'"—to the old home, to the lakeside, to the birds and trees, to the little church in the wilderness, to the friends of bygone days, to the childhood of the children, to the years of love, to the rest and quiet! She could not tell all she meant, but it is plain enough—the breaking forth of unutterable affection, the longing to hold back for one dear moment the darkening of time's twilight, the flood of sympathy, love and anxiety for husband, sons and daughters, the cry of the turning tide and the drooping wind. But God had for her better things than even these precious things of earth. The ebb of life went

on. Loved ones wept. The angels came—and they carried her away.

As I utter these words I think of the hold which the truth of immortality had upon her, as it must needs have upon all who consider life and its future. No sermons affected her more than did such as set forth the hope of glory, and told of the good things which God hath prepared for them that love Him. For her there was a blessed home, a sweet country, a heavenly Jerusalem, such as this world had never known and so long as time endures can never know. The grave is not the end; beyond its gloom lies the endless light—the joy and the rest which they have who behold the sea and the river, clear as crystal, shaded by rare and wondrous trees and bordered by the sweet and pleasant flowers and the streets of pure gold. In that dear land, the glory of which the richest imagination can only faintly suggest, the blessed inhabitants thereof, untouched by sorrow or sin, shall enjoy precious intercourse one with another, and above all else shall see the King in His beauty. This is the joy of heaven—to see God. All else is as nothing compared with Him. No more seeing through a glass darkly; but face to face. With

this assurance we know that it is not death which comes to the Christian in the moment when the eyes behold no more the things of earth; it is an apotheosis—a transformation of the humanity of the lower life into the vigor and splendor of the heavenly—a breaking of clouds, of clay, of bounds, and the rush of the soul, mightier than though lifted by eagle's wings, to freedom, light, saintship, gladness, and the presence of the Infinite and Eternal. And they sing sweet songs in yonder kingdom which make amends for all the tears of this world— songs like the sound of many waters, full and limitless and free; and the ebb and the night never come, but the flow and the day continue ever, bringing joys and creating pleasures, the very thought of which might well make us wish that we too were there. This hope which had been our departed one's gladness for many a long year, which stirred her heart to its deepest depths, is now for her a reality. The angels came—and they carried her away.

Good reason is there for having this service on this day. The festival of St. John the Baptist has been observed ever in this parish; and on this day, for years past, Mrs. Lucas loved to

gather her friends around her. And good reason, too, is there that I should have sought thus to set before you both the work and the character of this beloved and favored woman. Her example is worthy of emulation, her memory of most loving care. If I have spoken more fully of ideals, say, of womanhood and of the Church, it is partly because she delighted in such, and partly because without doing so I could not fairly suggest, much less display, her life. I do not suppose even now that I have said all that ought to be said. You will, however, bear me witness that I have nowhere exaggerated her great gifts or her remarkable virtues, and nowhere have I given praise that you know full well she did not deserve. The world is poorer for her loss. They who mourn her as a wife or as a mother will indeed find that her place can never be filled, but they will also discover comfort in the recollection of her useful life. They will remember instances of her kindliness of spirit, of her generosity of love, of her gentle and wise counsel, which others know nothing of. They will recall, as time goes on, traits of disposition and deeds of sweetness that will endear to them still more her memory. They

will think of her more tenderly, more deeply, more fondly, in the coming years, when the flow of grief has been stayed and the bitterness of bereavement has passed away. She will be to her children a restraining influence: they will remember her, and will stay ere they speak the word or do the deed that would bring dishonor to her name; they will remember her, and seek to prove themselves worthy of such a mother. And to her children's children she will become an ideal, a vision of glory, an illustration of many virtues—sacred, picturesque, inspiring, helpful. A wise and good woman, her grace was above gold.

The eventide comes on and the shadows lengthen fast. Now, as we sing our hymn, mellow and tender thoughts enter our soul— subdued, unutterable, full of saddest, sweetest melancholy. Soon shall the long summer day be ended, and in the sky shall appear the silent stars. In the night that draweth nigh, peace shall fall upon the weary children of earth; but to-morrow comes God's day—promise of the rest that remaineth. Therefore Hope, like a kind, good angel, tarries with us—and to these dear friends, who in the gathering

twilight have lost sight of her whom they love, Hope whispers comforting assurances: the souls of the righteous are in the hand of God; they are in peace; the care of them is with the Most High; "therefore shall they receive a glorious kingdom, and a beautiful crown from the Lord's hand: for, with His right hand shall He cover them, and with His arm shall He protect them." In that blessed country where she is gone—where night never comes, and where the wind breathes against the angels' robes—she shall be led on from glory to glory, until, in the Resurrection, God shall give her back again to her own, resplendent in the everlasting beauty, and happy in the everlasting life.

God, of His infinite mercy, grant to us, dear brethren, that in the day when men shall lay us with our feet towards the dawn, and the surpliced priest commits our body to the keeping of the earth, we may enter into the rest which we believe to be the heritage of this good woman—beside whose grave, with reverence and affection, as the flowers of remembrance drop from my hand, I say, "Her grace was above gold."

PRESS OF
TIMES PRINTING HOUSE
PHILADELPHIA

## Addenda.

The following was received too late to be printed in this volume:

Transcript of the Minutes, as recorded at the Memorial Service, held at the Assembly Room, Woman's Building, Chicago, August 2, 1893.

Mary E. McCandless, of Pennsylvania, submitted the following Memorial Resolutions for record:

"But three days after the meeting of the Board of Lady Managers, May 5th, last, Harriet Anne Lucas surrendered her soul to God. High and low, rich and poor, were alike to her. Mourned as she is by the community in which she lived, their grief is but a faint echo of the sorrow that crushes her household.

"A devoted wife, a loving mother, a true friend, she endeared herself to the Board of Lady Managers by her personal magnetism, her uniform gentleness, pleasing suavity, kindness

of heart and charming courtesy. Especially was she beloved by the Auxiliary Committees of Pennsylvania, who felt that the Chairman of the Committee of Woman's Work was a true woman, who was just to all and considered the interest of the entire State, and was in thorough harmony with the most remote committee.

"The Pennsylvania Exhibit of Woman's Work is her best monument, and each new panegyric uttered in its praise is another line added to her epitaph. To her colleagues, who relied on her sound judgment and advice, her loss is irreparable. If the blessings of her friends and neighbors were flowers her grave would be in perpetual bloom."

www.ingramcontent.com/pod-product-compliance
Lightning Source LLC
Chambersburg PA
CBHW020356030726
47496CB00007B/2157

9 783337 120856